The Eunuch

A Dark Tale

Richard Bird

Cerberus Books
San Antonio, Texas

A Softcover Original

Second Edition

Published by

Cerberus Books
San Antonio, Texas

ISBN-13: 978-0964647138
ISBN-10: 0964647133

Library of Congress Catalogue Number: 95-68970

Manufactured in the United States of America

FOR MAC

Hence, loathed Melancholy,
Of Cerberus and blackest Midnight born,
In Stygian cave forlorn,
'Mongst horrid shapes, and shrieks, and sights unholy . . . .

from *L'Allegro*
by John Milton, 1608-1674

ONE

When Nathan Doering first encountered Lucinda Webb in the sun-dappled erotic sculpture courtyard of the Dallas Gallery of Modern Art, he sported only one testicle, having lost its twin to a virulent attack of mumps in adolescence.

Twenty minutes later on Lucinda's king-size waterbed, Nathan, at the vulnerable age of forty-seven, was violently stripped of his precious remaining gonad and set upon a course that would drastically alter and, at last, give true meaning to his life.

* * * * *

Nathan had caught Lucinda's eye as he peered at her between the heavily muscled legs of a monstrous bronze statue of a nude woman. Lucinda was sitting on a bench with her sack lunch and had just taken a hungry bite from her tuna fish sandwich when she noticed Nathan stooping behind the statue, staring at her. His pale face was framed perfectly by the softly rounded inner thighs of the statue. From Lucinda's foreshortened perspective, the sculpture's grotesquely exaggerated labia majora appeared to be nestled on top of his blond head.

Startled, amused, fascinated—but unflappable—Lucinda swallowed and blankly returned his stare, her face immobile except for the pink flash of her tongue as she licked mayonnaise from her lips.

Nathan was smitten.

He stood up and sauntered around the statue, briefcase in hand, watching her from the corner of his eye. He moved obliquely toward her, first one way then the other, like a tacking sailboat.

Lucinda watched him coolly, sizing him up as he sidled closer. Average build. Not muscular, but toned. Fit. Mid-thirties, she guessed. But as Nathan tacked and rounded a quasi-cubist scrap metal representation of male genitalia, a shaft of sunlight struck and reflected from his scalp, only partially diffused by his thinning hair. Make that mid-forties, Lucinda noted, as Nathan squinted in the sun, revealing telltale crow's-feet around his eyes.

Nathan shifted his heavy briefcase to his left hand and loosened his necktie as he nonchalantly surveyed the sculpture garden. Imperceptibly (he thought) his eyes freeze-framed Lucinda's crossed, sheer black nylon-sheathed legs, then continued scanning the gallery courtyard. But this surreptitious voyeurism was not imperceptible to Lucinda.

Lucinda Webb was an expert in two disciplines: Art and Men. And she pursued both interests passionately. Thirty-four years old and still unmarried, she was a legend in the Texas avant-garde art community. Not as an artist. Not even as an art critic. But as a prophetess. Lucinda's special gift was her uncanny ability to recognize incipient genius. She had built her reputation and her fortune by discovering unknown male artists with inchoate ideas and techniques and then developing them into darlings of the Texas cutting-edge cultural scene.

Nathan tacked again and cruised down the path in front of the bench where Lucinda sat. He pretended not to notice her, though she gazed steadily at him.

"Hi, stranger," Lucinda said. Her voice was low, soft, and coy— her best Lauren Bacall imitation. "Come here often?"

Nathan was caught off guard. The slightly mocking humor in Lucinda's tone disarmed him, embarrassed him. He stopped and looked at her, blushing. She was unquestionably the most attractive human being he had ever seen. At close range now he could see that she was not really beautiful. Not even pretty. But there was a fullness, an earthy fecundity about her. In a word, she was erotic.

"No. Actually I've never been here," Nathan said. "Until now, that is. I was just walking by . . . and I . . . . It's a beautiful setting."

"Thanks," Lucinda said, smiling, looking straight up into his eyes. She took another big bite from her sandwich.

Nathan looked away. "Why are you thanking me? Do you work here?"

"I own this gallery. And everything in it," Lucinda mumbled with her mouth full.

"Oh." Nathan looked back at her. She was still staring at him, chewing. He self-consciously lowered his eyes and found himself looking through the gap of her loose, black silk, scoop-necked blouse. Lucinda was bra-less. From his vantage point above her he could see her entire right breast and all but the nipple of her left one. Her breasts were not large or plump like melons, but were exquisitely elongated, curving up in sensuous arcs like fat, ripe bananas. They were tropical breasts. Jungle breasts. *National Geographic* breasts.

Nathan's knees buckled, but he adroitly covered his loss of composure by quickly bending to put his briefcase down on the flagstone pathway. He cleared his throat.

"May I sit on your bench?" His voice was strained, about half an octave higher than normal. He felt a bit dizzy.

"Sure, go ahead," Lucinda said huskily. "But keep your hands to yourself."

Nathan let slip a nervous giggle, then caught himself. He suddenly

3

felt thirteen again, in the middle of a pubescent sexual fantasy. A gentle breeze wafted Lucinda's body scent to him, a breeze warm and humid, laden with mysterious spices and salt, like tropical sea air at night. He closed his eyes and inhaled deeply. He sensed that something extraordinary was about to happen. He let himself go.

"I think you are a strange woman," he said.

"Do you like strange women?" Lucinda's voice sounded deep and dangerous.

"Yes. I do."

"Do you like my tits?"

Nathan's heart palpitated, then began to pound furiously. "Oh, God, yes! Yes, I do," he said. "I have only dreamed of . . . of . . . ."

"If you promise not to say another word, I will make your dreams come true," Lucinda said.

"I . . . ."

"Not a word! Not till it's over!" Lucinda stood up, leaving her unfinished tuna fish sandwich and lunch sack on the bench, and took Nathan's hand firmly. "Come with me. Hurry!" Nathan stood, dazed, electrified, and followed Lucinda out of the courtyard and down the sunny sidewalk past fern bars, boutiques, and other art galleries toward the fashionable urban residential enclave where she lived with a Boston terrier named Baby Bow Wow.

Lucinda was in a state of extreme sexual anticipation. This was not the first time she had initiated spontaneous, impromptu sex with a stranger. It was never something she planned. It just seemed to happen now and then. The circumstances had to be just right. The man had to be reasonably good-looking. He had to be clean. But, above all, he had to be manageable. To determine this last quality, she relied purely on gut instinct. Lucinda knew in her gut that Nathan was manageable.

In her nubile teenage masturbatory fantasies, the men . . . or boys . . . had always been faceless. They never spoke. They had no personalities. To personify the incubus was to break the spell.

As a young high school virgin, her first real sexual opportunity, in the back seat of a '61 Chevy convertible under the stars, fizzled. Her boyfriend talked it to death. By the time he got up the gumption to act, Lucinda was irked and out of the mood. Because the personality quirks of her familiar male schoolmates invariably cooled her passion, she remained chaste until her senior year at North Texas State University, where she majored in art and minored in business administration.

That last year in college, on the first day of the second term in a drawing class, she met a new transfer student, a handsome but sullen red-headed boy in a torn heavy metal T-shirt with the sleeves ripped off to the armpits. He slouched in his seat and stared at her for an entire hour rather than study the nude model posing at the front of the classroom.

When the class adjourned, he followed her to the deserted gymnasium where they had grunting, but otherwise silent, athletic sex on a tattered wrestling mat under the darkened bleachers. For Lucinda, it was an exhilarating and formative experience. A real eye-opener. The red-headed boy was arrested the following day for selling marijuana on campus.

She never saw him again.

Lucinda walked rapidly down the sidewalk, though the length of her stride was limited by her tight, but stylish, Neiman Marcus black silk skirt. She quickened her pace to synchronize the sharp cadence of her high-heeled pumps on the pavement with the throbbing of her heart. Lucinda had rhythm.

Nathan, still holding her hand, lagged behind, occasionally stumbling as he followed the cynosure of her undulating buttocks. Lucinda watched her buttocks, too. She continually glanced at her reflection in the plate glass windows of the shops, restaurants, and office buildings they passed. An admirer had once told her that her ass was "like little animals" when she walked. "Like two jack rabbits in a gunnysack," he'd said. He was a cowboy. Lucinda, watching her reflection, was inclined to agree. She believed her round, protruding, high-slung cheeks to be her best physical attribute, though she realized that her oddly-shaped breasts were also an irresistible attraction to certain idiosyncratic men. Like the one following her now.

Nathan was hyperventilating. He fought for control. He could not remember ever having been so aroused. Well, perhaps once. When he was a seventeen-year-old virgin in Richmond, Virginia, he had worked as a sales clerk in a Thom McAn shoe store after school. A long-legged woman with pitch-black pubic hair worked there, too, and they often found themselves together retrieving or restocking shoe boxes on the highest shelves in the narrow-aisled stockroom.

The woman, who was married to the store manager, used a steep, castered ladder to reach the top few shelves. Nathan, a courteous youth, would steady the ladder for her. One day he noticed that she had forgotten to wear her usual pink lace panties. That's how he came to know the color of her pubic hair.

Stunned by his first astonishing close-up view of an actual vulva, Nathan stood transfixed, unable to move aside as she descended the ladder. The hem of her full skirt floated over his head. She paused, trembling. Nathan could hear her breathing, and he could hear the ladder rattle gently on its casters. Otherwise, it was very quiet under her skirt.

She tentatively descended another step, until her bare buttocks brushed against Nathan's nose. A brave lad, he held his ground. As slowly as a petal unfolds from a flower in the sun, she arched her back and reached out to Nathan. At last he responded and plunged his callow face into that dark and oleaginous orifice till lips met succulent lips.

The woman shrieked. The ladder scooted. And all came crashing down in a heap. Nathan's head came to rest between the proverbial rock (the concrete floor) and a hard place (the bone that forms the mons veneris). His nose was broken, his lips were split open, and his upper front teeth were temporarily loosened. He was knocked out cold.

Upon hearing the commotion, the manager rushed in from the sales floor to find his wife sitting on his clerk's face. Several curious customers had a peek as well. The manager charged in a rage. Nathan came to just in time, narrowly escaped and never returned. The manager never mailed his commission check, which would have been a considerable amount, for Nathan was a productive salesman.

The experience, however, had been worth the loss. He had finally had sex, after a fashion. But most important, he had, in that one brief, sweet kiss, acquired a lifelong taste for cunnilingus . . . that most intimate and passionate form of human communication.

Over the ensuing years, Nathan had worked diligently to elevate his specialized communications skills to a high degree of art. Though he worked professionally as a copy machine salesman, he considered himself an artist.

Lucinda led Nathan, breathless, deep into the city's Downtown Arts District, past the formidable Dallas Museum of Art toward the spanking new and cavernous Morton H. Myerson Symphony Center, which cost taxpayers and wealthy private patrons a whopping $200,000,000.00. The homeless people who slept and urinated on its sweeping steps and broad verandas were not allowed admission without a ticket. And a bath.

Between the two megalithic buildings, each of which occupied its own entire city block (not counting acres of adjacent dedicated parking lots on prime real estate) stood an anachronism billed by the Dallas Chamber of Commerce as "a bold experiment in alternative urban lifestyles": eighty-seven pre-fab pseudo-Victorian two-story condominiums, crammed cheek by jowl onto still another entire city block. Each condo came complete with pastel vinyl siding, Lexan windows divided by fake stick-on plastic muntins to look like old-fashioned wooden double-hung windows, injection molded plastic gingerbread trim, a white low-maintenance polyvinyl chloride picket fence, and a Lilliputian lawn. At $250,000.00 a pop, they sold like popcorn. Lucinda had been one of the first to snap one up.

She led Nathan to a locked gate in the eight-foot high iron security fence that surrounded the enclave. Nathan noticed a small brass sign on the fence next to the gate. It was engraved:

LA COTERIE
Arts District Living Centre
Phase I
Private
Residents and Guests Only

Above the sign was a surveillance video camera pointed right at him. He turned his back on the camera and watched Lucinda punch her security entrance code number on a ten-key pad next to the gate. Her hands were shaking. Nathan had an obvious erection, which he covered with his briefcase.

The computer-controlled electronic gate slowly opened, and they entered, stepping back in time to the reign of Queen Victoria.

Lucinda's gingerbread condo was near the gate. A pale yellow one. It was sandwiched between a blue one and a beige one. The pattern—blue, yellow, beige—repeated itself every three condos in uniform, unalterable, vinyl perpetuity: eighty-seven fake, pastel plastic grandmother houses in neat rows covering one square block of priceless downtown Dallas real estate . . . a block that was surrounded by obscenely expensive monuments to patrons of the arts, which in turn were surrounded by towering glass and steel cloud-penetrating erections to the glory of Dallas businessmen.

"Big **D**, little **a**, double **l**, **a**, **s**," Nathan sang to himself.

Lucinda unlocked her front door and stepped into her living room where she was greeted by Baby Bow Wow, a randy little black and white Boston terrier who immediately began hunching her leg. Baby Bow Wow had an erection, too.

"Get away! You disgusting little rat!" Lucinda hissed. She kicked at him, and he scampered out of the room, yelping, his little claws clicking on the polished hardwood floor. Nathan noted with interest that the dog possessed inordinately large testicles. As Baby Bow Wow skidded around the corner into the hallway, he watched . . . as if in slow motion . . . how its balls bobbled between its muscular hind legs, like two Ping-Pong balls in a tight, shiny, black satin sack.

Lucinda looked down at her leg. Her stocking had been snagged by the dog's front paws where he had clutched her. She looked at Nathan, then down at the bulge in his pants.

"Come on," she said, starting up the staircase to her bedroom.

"But no talking." Nathan followed, like a randy dog, still carrying his briefcase.

Lucinda started undressing at the top of the stairs. By the time she reached the foot of her king-size waterbed and turned to face Nathan, she was stripped down to a black, lacy garter belt and stockings. Her legs were long and slender, and her pubic hair was as black . . . as black as . . . . From the waist down she could have passed for the manager's wife at the Thom McAn shoe store.

Nathan dropped his briefcase and seized a banana breast in each hand. He held on as Lucinda quickly and deftly untied his tie, unbuttoned his shirt, unbuckled his belt, and unzipped his trousers. In the twinkling of an eye her hand slipped through his fly and under his shorts. She slid her hand down the shaft of his penis, grabbed his solitary testicle, and gave it a wicked squeeze.

Nathan winced. He searched her eyes for any sign that she might have noticed his missing part. Lucinda smiled at him salaciously, then stooped to remove his trousers, shorts, shoes, and socks. As she rose, Nathan knelt. He cradled her pooky buttocks in his hands and nuzzled her bushy, black triangle.

Lucinda sighed a long, deep sigh and fell back on the gurgling waterbed, throwing her silkened legs up high and wide. Whereupon, Nathan, the artist, went to work.

He wielded his talented tongue and lips as a painter wields his brush and palette, as a sculptor wields his chisel and mallet. Like a brilliant conductor he directed Lucinda's clitoris with his glossal baton, inspiring her to symphonic orgasm, building her pianissimo little cries and whimpers of pleasure to a crescendo of forte animal grunts, then to a moaning tutta forza, and finally to a climactic, blood-curdling, screaming coda.

Lucinda's alarming scream of passion segued to an even more

alarming snarling and growling that closed rapidly on Nathan's posterior. A sudden, excruciating pain in the scrotum! Another bloodcurdling scream! This time from Nathan as he leapt to his feet. Baby Bow Wow, his jaws locked like a vise, dangled and writhed in the air between Nathan's legs, snarling and jerking his head violently from side to side like a puppy playing tug of war with a squeak toy.

"JESUS!" Nathan screamed, swatting fecklessly at the dog. "Get him off! Get him OFF me!"

"Baby Bow Wow! NO!" shouted Lucinda. "Bad dog!"

Baby Bow Wow gave one last cruel snap of his head and dropped to the floor on all fours. He swallowed. He gagged. And then he retched, finally regurgitating Nathan's one and only last testicle onto Lucinda's antique Early American hooked rug.

Nathan passed out.

TWO

On the way to the hospital, Nathan remained essentially unconscious. There was little loss of blood, and his injury wasn't even especially painful—just a sort of burning, stinging sensation between his legs where his scrotum had been shredded, and shucked, so to speak, by Baby Bow Wow's sharp little teeth. But there was a dull, indefinite ache somewhere in his pelvic area that he couldn't pinpoint, an elusive ache that seemed to ebb and flow in a slow, amorphous throb. Again and again he would momentarily come to, only to feel that phantom throb, remember what had happened, then faint dead away once more, slumping on the Windsor blue leather seat of Lucinda's new turbo Saab as it sped northward toward Parkland Memorial Hospital—the very same hospital where John F. Kennedy had been taken when he was assassinated in downtown Dallas.

The emergency staff, unfortunately, had not been able to save Kennedy in 1963, despite the miracles of space-age technology. But Lucinda fervently hoped they *would* be able to save *this* man . . . whoever he was.

After all, this *was* 1991. Space technology was now practically "low-tech" compared with today's medical wizardry and the modern miracles of the artificial life extension industry, which just happened to be a very hot industry in Big D. If they can keep brain-dead octogenarians kicking indefinitely against everyone's wishes and better judgment, thought Lucinda, then they certainly should be able to sew the life-giving seed pod back onto a man who enjoys life—a man who by all rights should go on living, enjoying, and giving joy in return. The thought gave Lucinda a little tingle. She touched her Gucci purse on the seat beside her, where she had stashed Nathan's testicle, on ice in a Ziploc bag.

"Hey!" Lucinda shouted, as Nathan's eyes rolled back in their sockets again for the umpteenth time. "What's your name? Tell me your NAME! TELL—ME—YOUR—NAME!" She remembered from a first aid and CPR class she had taken that one must try to keep a shock victim conscious if at all possible. She also realized how awkward it could be bringing a man in his condition to the Parkland Trauma Center when she didn't even know his name.

"Name! WHAT—IS—YOUR—NAME?"

"Nathan . . . Doering," slurred Nathan thickly.

"Nothin' doing? Don't give me that crap!" snapped Lucinda. "I need to know your *name*! Speak to me! I'm taking you to the hospital! Do you want to die before we even get there?"

"Yes," said Nathan.

Lucinda careened her car into the hospital's emergency ambulance area and screeched to a stop at the curb. She jumped out yelling.

"Help! Help! A man is dying in my car!"

Two large, black male attendants in snow-white uniforms dashed to the car with a stretcher and opened the passenger door. Nathan was out cold again.

"Whasamatta wif him?" one of the attendants asked. "Wha' happen'?"

"He . . . ah . . . an amputation!" Lucinda said.

"Amputation?" He looked at Nathan, perplexed.

"He ain' missin' no arms. He gots his legs," the other attendant

13

said, equally perplexed. "I don' see no blood."

"You be jivin' us, Lady?"

"Trust me," Lucinda said evenly. "You will understand when you take his pants off."

"Shee-yit!" said one attendant.

"Muh-fuh!" said the other.

"Now," said Lucinda, glaring at them, "will you move your ass before he dies in my car?"

The attendants wheeled Nathan into Parkland's famous triage holding tank, through a crowd of victims with stab wounds, gunshot wounds, beer bottle and baseball bat wounds, broken arms, smashed legs, cuts and contusions, nosebleeds, and broken teeth—all queued up for the latest in free miracle medical technology. Parkland! County Hospital! The People's Hospital! The Hospital With A Heart! A Mecca for the indigent. A haven for the miserable of Dallas County. Straight through this teeming mass of human suffering they pushed Nathan on the stretcher.

"Look out!" yelled one attendant, shoving aside a man with a filthy, bloody shirt wrapped around his head.

"Y'all MOVE it!" bellowed the other. "Dis boy done loss his dong!"

The traumatized crowd, as if responding to the voice of God, parted like the Red Sea.

In the examining room, a nurse who looked like a weight lifter came at Nathan with a pair of surgical scissors and proceeded to cut his trousers off his body.

"Why don't you just unzip them and *take* them off?" Lucinda asked.

"We *cut* all garments off *here*, Miss," the nurse said curtly. "We can't risk complicating the injury."

"You gon *scare* dat boy to deaf he wake up see you doin' dat cuttin'," said one of the attendants.

The nurse looked around angrily. "What are you two doing in here? Get back to triage! Now!" She went back to work.

Suddenly Nathan came to. He saw, and heard, the big scissors snip-snipping up his pant leg toward his crotch. "Yiiiiiiiii!!!" he screamed, then promptly passed out again.

"I tol' you!" cried the attendant.

"Out!" shouted the nurse, continuing to cut away Nathan's pants, belt, and finally his shorts. The attendants hovered outside, peeking around the door, trying to get a firsthand glimpse of their worst nightmare. With a rubber-gloved finger the nurse flopped Nathan's penis back on his abdomen, exposing his lacerated, empty sack.

"I thought you say he done cut his dong off!" exclaimed one of the attendants.

"You said that. I didn't," Lucinda replied icily.

"OUT!!" shouted the weight lifter nurse again. She slammed the door in their faces, then turned and looked accusingly at Lucinda. "What in God's name happened to this man?"

"I . . . he . . . it . . . ." Lucinda flushed and stammered. "It . . . it . . . was a . . . freak accident. He . . . ah . . . he fell."

"Fell?" The nurse was incredulous.

"Her goddamn dog bit my nut off!" cried Nathan from the stretcher. He was fully conscious now. "He ate it! At least I think he ate it." Nathan stared at the ceiling, as if trying to remember.

"No! I have it!" Lucinda said excitedly, rooting in her Gucci purse for the Ziploc bag. "It's right here!" She produced the bag with its gruesome contents and dangled it over Nathan's face so he could see it. "Baby Bow Wow spit it up! I saved it for you!"

"Jesus!" said Nathan. He closed his eyes.

"Jesus wept!" said the nurse. "Get that thing away!" She bent over Nathan and began to gingerly examine his scrotum. "Uh-oh," she said. Gravely, she looked up into Nathan's eyes. He was up on his elbows trying to get a look at the damage.

"Sir," said the nurse in her best bad news voice, "I'm sorry to inform you that *both* of your testicles are missing."

"I only had one," Nathan said, tearing up. "It was . . . the only one I had left. Jesus!" He fell back on the stretcher, coiling into a fetal position, and began to sob piteously.

"Holy Mary, Mother of God," incanted the nurse as she crossed herself. "I'll get the urologist." She hurried out of the room, leaving Lucinda holding the bag, and Nathan trying to weep his way back to the womb.

While the nurse was out, Lucinda comforted Nathan, calmed him down, extracted his name. She told him hers and apologized profusely for Baby Bow Wow's abominable behavior.

"I'm going to kill that fucking dog," Nathan said.

"Nathan, Nathan," Lucinda pleaded. She tried to reason with him. "He's just a dog! You're a man! Baby Bow Wow only did what any dog would have done under the circumstances. He thought you were hurting me. Naturally he would attack!"

"Why did you have to scream like that?" Nathan asked bitterly. His loins throbbed, vaguely.

"I couldn't help it," Lucinda said in a voice almost like a little girl's. She lowered her eyes demurely, and gently squeezed his hand. "You made me scream like that."

Nathan, despite his pain, his grief, his ineffable sense of loss, still couldn't help noticing, again, what an unbelievably attractive woman Lucinda was. And sweet, as well.

"You're not going to sue me, are you, Nathan?" Lucinda

asked sweetly.

Nathan laughed, then grimaced. "No, no," he said, trying to ignore the sudden stabbing pain in his crotch that laughing produced. "It takes a lawyer to sue, and I hate lawyers worse than that . . . that . . . STUPID, GODDAMN, FUCKING, ASSHOLE DOG OF YOURS!" He started to sob again, just as Dr. Peter Smith, the urologist, walked in.

Dr. Smith closed the door, quickly, quietly, and came over to Nathan, placing one soft, warm, doctor hand gently on his forehead and the other on his shoulder.

"Pull yourself together, my boy," he said in his best Marcus Welby imitation, although, as Lucinda noted, he was a good deal younger than Nathan. "It's not the end of the world, believe me," he added reassuringly. "I am Dr. Peter Smith, and I am here to help you."

Lucinda liked him immediately, though she couldn't understand why. He was scrawny and sallow-faced with a beaked nose, stringy red hair, bloodshot blue eyes, and a posture like a flamingo. And he had a peculiar, yet not altogether disagreeable, odor.

Nathan instantly disliked him. Intensely. "Get your hands off me," he said to the doctor.

"I'm sorry. I was only trying to comfort you."

"I don't want comfort. I want my ball."

Lucinda reached in her Gucci bag and brought out the Ziplocked, iced testicle again. She presented it to Dr. Smith. "Can you sew it back on?" she asked hopefully.

Dr. Smith held the bag up to the light and examined its contents. "Hmmmm," he hummed. Then he probed Nathan's barren, lifeless scrotum. "Hmmmm. Where's the other one?" he asked, looking at Lucinda. Lucinda shrugged and looked at Nathan.

"I had a bad case of mumps when I was a kid. It dried up and

17

went away," Nathan said blackly.

"Hmmmm."

"Well? Can you do it? Can you sew it back on?" Lucinda asked again.

"I'm afraid that would be impossible," Dr. Smith answered. He handed the bag back to Lucinda.

"Impossible?" Lucinda cried. "ImPOSSible? This is 1991, for Christ's sake! We've put a man on the moon! Surely we can put a little testicle on a man! Look!" She help up the Ziploc bag. "I've kept it cold! It hasn't died yet!"

"Forget it, Lucinda!" Nathan blubbered. He had been listening to her vain appeal with his eyes shut, sobbing again. "Forget it! It's useless. Take it home and put it in your refrigerator. Or feed it to Baby Bow Wow. I'm sure he would enjoy a little TREAT! Yeah! Feed it to that vicious, voracious little fucking rat you call a dog and I hope he fucking CHOKES on it. I'm gonna KILL that ASSHOLE SONOFABITCH IF ITS THE LAST THING I EVER DO!!!" Nathan recoiled again into a fetal position, his shuddering, pitiful sobs causing his stretcher to wobble and rattle gently on its casters.

Dr. Smith motioned to Lucinda, and they went out of the examining room and closed the door.

The gentle rattle of the stretcher casters had a calming effect on Nathan. The sound evoked memories of that magical day, so many years ago, at the Thom McAn shoe store when the long-legged wife of the manager had tentatively . . . oh, so tentatively descended that castered ladder in the stockroom, trembling like a frightened . . . like a frightened what . . .? Like a frightened, pantiless, long-legged, black-bushed Thom McAn shoe store manager's wife about to get her pussy kissed by a seventeen-year-old, horny, red-blooded, virgin, all-American boy! That's what!

Cunnilingus is a dangerous art, thought Nathan as he drifted off into a dreamless, childlike sleep.

Lucinda and Dr. Peter Smith, the urologist, conferred out in the hall as Nathan slept. They filled out forms. Lucinda supplied Nathan's name (which she now knew), his address (she gave hers), his age (she guessed), and his occupation (Artist!).

Dr. Smith told Lucinda ("May I call you Lucinda?" "Why, yes. Of course, Doctor." "Peter. Please." "All right. Peter.") that he would have to hospitalize Nathan for a few days for observation ("Psychological as well as physical, if you know what I mean, Lucinda." "Of course, Peter. I understand.") and that he would require a tetanus shot and, possibly, the very painful rabies antidote.

"Do you have any reason to think your dog is rabid, Lucinda? Was he foaming at the mouth or acting strangely either before or after the attack?"

"No. Absolutely not, Peter. He is very protected. He never goes outside the compound. He was just being a dog."

"Well, then, we'll hold off on the antidote unless I hear from you. Let me know, Lucinda, if you note any change in . . . . What did Nathan call him?"

"A vicious, voracious little . . . . Oh, silly me! His name is Baby Bow Wow!"

"Yes. Baby Bow Wow. Cute name."

"His real name is Yahweh."

"What?"

"Never mind. It's a long story. I'll tell you about it another time. By the way, Peter, what is that aftershave you're wearing?"

"Oh, it's a cologne. For men. It's called *Pierre: For Men*. Do you like it?"

"Yes. Very much. I wasn't sure at first, but I must say it is growing on me."

"I'm so glad."

"Well, I guess it's good-bye for now, then." Lucinda girlishly offered her hand, like a flower. Dr. Smith took it in both of his warm, clean, soft, well-manicured, doctor hands . . . gently, but firmly, as if to lovingly de-flower it. He gazed into her erotic brown eyes with his bloodshot blue ones.

"Yes, Lucinda. Good-bye. For now."

Lucinda turned, strangely aroused, and walked down the corridor toward Parkland's famous triage holding tank for the morbidly wounded uninsured citizens of the great city of Dallas. She was aware of her undulating buttocks, her "little animals" struggling to break out of their silken "gunnysack" as she walked. Dr. Peter Smith, the urologist, was aware, too, and she knew it. She raised her hand to her nose and sniffed it . . . the hand so recently caressed, and de-flowered, by the aromatic Dr. Smith. *Pierre: For Men.* She said the name to herself, silently, forming the words with her full, erotic lips. What an extraordinary odor, she thought, and what an extraordinary effect it has on me . . . for he is unquestionably the most unattractive man I have ever met in my life.

THREE

Lucinda visited Nathan often . . . as often as two or three times a day . . . during his week-long hospitalization. She usually saw Dr. Smith ("Peter. Please.") while she was in the room, because the good doctor, personally, took at least a dozen urine samples from Nathan every single day. "Best way to monitor his progress," he would explain cryptically. Nathan, morose and still in some pain, was inconvenienced and extremely irritated by this constant urinalysis.

"I hate that son of a bitch," Nathan said to Lucinda one day as the doctor happily left the room with yet another bottle of Nathan's urine. "He makes me drink gallons of water and juice and coffee and tea every day just so he can get more of my piss. But that's not why I hate him. I don't know why I hate him. All I can tell you is that every time he comes in here it's all I can do to keep from smashing in his pasty little face. I don't know why he enrages me like that. I can't put my finger on it."

"That is most peculiar, Nathan," Lucinda said, stroking his blond, curly hair.

"Yeah. And I'll tell you something else. I can't stand the way he smells."

Lucinda's ears pricked.

"I don't know what it is. He walks in here. I smell him. I get pissed off."

"I think it's his aftershave," Lucinda said, " . . . or cologne, actually. It's called *Pierre: For Men.*"

"How do you know that?"

"I asked him about it the day we came to the emergency room."

"Yeah. I remember smelling it then, too, and I got pissed off at him right away. The guy ought to change brands."

"Oh, I don't know, Nathan. I don't find it all that bad, really."

"Then you've got something wrong with your nose."

"Maybe there's something wrong with yours," said Lucinda with a good-natured smile.

Nathan and Lucinda grew very close, even loving, to each other during that week in the hospital. She brought him books and magazines to read, delivered his favorite meal from the delicatessen (grilled knackwurst on rye with mustard only, two bags of potato chips, and a Coke), and one day surprised him with a slab of chilled cheesecake topped with strawberries. She gave him massages in the dark, and sponged his body with cool water in the morning window light. She ran her fingers through his hair while looking deeply, seriously, into his dark blue eyes. She kissed him tenderly on his lips. She even hid behind the chair in his room one night after visiting hours till "lights out," then ripped off his pajamas like a wild woman and gave him a tongue bath. Nathan had responded to a state of semi-tumescence, but then went flaccid again when he thought, infuriatingly, of Baby Bow Wow.

"I don't mind, Nathan," Lucinda had said, and she meant it. "It makes me happy just to lick you . . . any way you are . . . and to have you lick me."

"Why are you being so nice to me? I'm going to kill your pet."

"Because you are an artist."

"I think it's because you feel guilty. You feel sorry for me, and you feel a responsibility because your dog castrated me."

Lucinda vehemently denied this, although she knew there was some truth to what he said. Yet, she thought, who can say where the line is drawn between guilt and love, compassion and passion, responsibility and adoration?

Nathan told her stories of his childhood in Virginia, where he had felt happy and carefree in the '40's, idealistic and confident in the '50's, confused and disillusioned in the '60's. And he told her about the '70's, when his young, tenuous life had begun to unravel after his marriage had ended in divorce. He told her about his demons, his dreams, his disappointments. He told anecdotes, strange tales, lies. He told the truth. He left out the darkest nights. He embellished, he exaggerated, he fabricated. He told her jokes, he posed conundrums, he recited some of his own bad poetry. He confessed to her his deepest secrets. He made her laugh. He made her cry. And then he told her he loved her.

Lucinda asked him to come and live with her for a while. She said she wanted to take care of him, to nurture him, to nurse him back to wholeness.

Nathan accepted.

During that bittersweet, confusing, frightening week, with his emotions swinging crazily from romantic euphoria to the nadir of personal despair, Nathan learned as much about Lucinda as he had told her about himself. He learned of her low self-esteem and her painful lack of self-confidence as a child growing up in Corpus Christi under the overprotective, fearful, hyper-critical influence of a fundamentalist Baptist family . . . a family scared shitless of offending their wrathful, vengeful, mean-spirited God, terrified of burning in the damnation of hell for all eternity . . . a family who, because of this very fear, were rendered so emotionally tight-ass that they could not love, truly love, their neighbors . . . or even themselves. Demonstrative love was taboo in Lucinda's family, and she was scarred by its absence.

She told Nathan about her prolonged virginity. He listened to two solid hours of convoluted, agonizing self-analysis on why she thought she couldn't love a man . . . "Never have, can't now, never will," she'd concluded with conviction. She talked another hour about how she couldn't really and truly *enjoy* sex unless it was anonymous. She referred again and again to her "anonymity fetish," their own meeting in her gallery courtyard being "a case in point." She berated herself for her immorality, her cold-heartedness. She bragged that she was perhaps the only truly independent, liberated woman in Dallas . . . a happy, self-sufficient woman. She said she used men at her pleasure. Men were mere playthings to her. "Just dildos with wallets," she'd said. "Well, I've got my own wallet now, and I can go out and *buy* myself the best damn dildo on the market if I want to! Who needs men? Not me, Buddy!" Then she broke down and collapsed in Nathan's arms, weeping. Her cries came from a place very far away, or very long ago. Nathan held her, and she cried herself to sleep.

Nathan had to work to get the low-down on eunuch-hood. Dr. Smith counseled him, in a fragmented way, on the ins and outs of castration, answering one or two questions on each of his frequent urine runs before hurriedly leaving with the goods. Nathan was happy to learn, after some tough questioning, that with regular testosterone injections life could continue pretty much as usual.

"Of course, you will no longer be able to procreate," Dr. Smith said.

Nathan felt a pang of nostalgia as he thought of his daughter Rose, his only child, who had been cruelly taken from him by his wife when she had walked out of their marriage twenty-five years earlier. After the divorce, she had married her lawyer, and Nathan had lost all visitation rights. Permanently. Just three years old at the time, Rose had been the light of his life.

"I'm a little old to be having children," Nathan said.

"Before long, you'll forget you even *had* balls," Dr. Smith said cheerily.

"Ball," corrected Nathan.

Nathan wanted to know the source of the testosterone with which he would be injected.

"Well, we used to extract it from the testes of bulls," Dr. Smith said, "but these days it is synthetically produced, and it's just as good. And a lot less expensive. Thank God for the miracles of modern medical science, eh, Nathan?"

"I'm sure the bulls are thankful," Nathan said.

Nathan did not sleep a wink the night that Lucinda surprised him with a tongue bath. His failure to rise to the occasion had caused him to lie awake, wide-eyed, worrying about impotence, until Dr. Smith made his seven o'clock urine run.

"There should be no *physiological* cause and effect between castration and impotence," Dr. Smith assured him, "as long as you take your testosterone shots."

Still unassured, Nathan hesitantly, euphemistically, told him of his inability to get an erection the preceding night despite the extraordinarily erotic stimulation provided by Lucinda.

"Did she attempt to perform fellatio upon you?" Dr. Smith

asked stiffly.

"She didn't just attempt. She did. And more. Much more," said Nathan. "But I never got an erection."

"That kind of behavior is strictly forbidden in this hospital," Dr. Smith said, his face flushing with anger. Nathan was angry with him, too, as always.

"I wouldn't worry about it at this point," said Dr. Smith as he stood up abruptly, a fresh urine sample in his hand. "You are no doubt still suffering psychological trauma from your . . . unfortunate accident. Everything should return to normal after you start your testosterone treatment, and as long as you don't become neurotically fixated on your loss."

"When can I start the shots?" Nathan asked eagerly.

"I'll let you know," said Dr. Smith. He left the room in a huff.

Nathan sent Lucinda on urgent errands to the library. He read everything she could find and bring to him on the subject of eunuchs, castration, impotence. From his reading and from the bits of information he could extract from Dr. Smith on his hourly urine raids, Nathan learned, first of all, that he was not alone in this world. There were literally thousands of human steers, at any given time in history, walking around, going about their business. No telling how many there were in Dallas alone. At this minute!

Wars, Nathan learned, are the primary producers of eunuchs: the occasional diabolically accurate sniper shot; the freak shard of shrapnel from an exploding grenade, mortar, or bomb; the snickersnack of the vorpal torture blade in prison camp interrogation rooms. Many geldings came home from Vietnam, and other wars, so many other wars, having suffered such bad luck. But the vast majority of war eunuchs were made by land mines. Mines can certainly kill and often do. But they are designed primarily to maim, to blow toes off, to make hamburger out of feet, to shatter kneecaps, to blind, to deafen, and yes, to castrate. The man who came up with the idea of land mines, thought Nathan, should be given a medal for sheer ingenuity in enemy intimidation and destruction of morale.

Nathan read of other, more curious, cases of castration . . . mostly accidental . . .

. . . of the obese and careless man who, while sitting on the toilet in a Mexican restaurant following a heavy meal, lit a cigarette and tossed the still flaming match between his legs; the ensuing muffled explosion cracked the porcelain commode and turned his tamales into refried beans.

. . . of the teenage boy in 1951 who, at what must have been a wild party, recklessly lit his own fart with a Zippo lighter; unfortunately his trousers, which were made of one of the early synthetic, permanent-press, highly flammable fabrics, burst into flames and cooked his taut, adolescent gonads like hard-boiled eggs. Some people will risk anything to be funny, thought Nathan.

. . . of the remorseful child molester in the Huntsville prison who mutilated himself with a spoon out of unspeakable grief, shame, and self-hatred. Life imprisonment was not, to this man, a sufficiently Draconian sentence; castration was, for *his* crime, the only condign punishment.

Nathan read with disbelief about a drunk who took a shit in a mop bucket and, thinking he was flushing a toilet, pushed down the squeeze-roller lever, ironing his bow wows into pancakes. His skepticism was justified, for he found the account of this bizarre accident in an obscure, picaresque first novel written in 1934 by a writer who was never heard from again.

Nathan was astonished to learn of the outrageous number of

premeditated and malicious castrations performed every year in the United States. According to statistics tabulated by a certain Arnold P. Skidmore in his doctoral dissertation, "The Psychology of Revenge," at the University of Texas at Austin, a staggering seven hundred and sixty-two documented cases of vengeful nut-cutting occurred in 1968 alone. Most of the mischief was done by crazed cuckolds. Other culprits included ordinary fathers avenging their daughters' dishonor, loan shark collectors, Ku Klux Klansmen, a couple of honest-to-god sex perverts, and one schizophrenic Middle Eastern exchange student who claimed Allah personally commanded him to castrate any American devil whom he considered to be a particularly dangerous infidel.

Significantly, reflected Nathan, only one scorned woman resorted to such fury. At least in 1968.

Of course, Nathan was already aware that potentates throughout history had routinely emasculated their slaves and servants for the pragmatic purpose of running efficient harems. And he knew that the ancient Romans often castrated their slaves to control their population. But what he did *not* know until he read it with horror, moral outrage, and righteous indignation, was that the Catholic Church, in its divine wisdom, ritualistically cut . . . CUT! . . . the balls off little boys in the Pope's choir to preserve, to the everlasting glory of Jesus Christ, the angelic voices of those innocent children.

So much for the steel-fisted papal position on planned parenthood, sneered Nathan.

But what's really scary, he thought, is that this church, which still controls the minds of millions upon millions of ignorant people who cannot or will not think for themselves, didn't raise its consciousness sufficiently to stop the mutilation until 1770. That was barely two hundred years ago . . . a mere blink of an eye in the evolution of the human brain.

Nathan sank into a deep depression.

One day Lucinda brought Nathan a quasi-medical tome entitled *I'm Joe's Genitals*. Nathan's irrational anxiety grew apace with his fertile imagination as he read that impotence is often a result of certain brain disorders—usually caused by head injury—in the hypothalamus, disorders that arrest the natural cascade of hormones from the brain to the pituitary gland to the adrenal glands, and finally to what everyone secretly believes to be man's true sexual nerve center. Nathan broke into a sweat. He had been knocked unconscious no less than eight times in his short, fragile life. He had, as they used to say in high school, a glass jaw.

As his desultory browsing in the book degenerated into perusing graphically descriptive passages on various venereal diseases and even genital cancer, Nathan became aware that the vague throbbing sensation in his pelvic region had gradually, over the last few days, become more focused. It seemed to be centered now in his rectum.

FOUR

On the day that Nathan was scheduled to be discharged from the hospital, Dr. Peter Smith, the urologist, failed to make his seven a.m. urine collection. Nor did he come at eight, nine, ten, or eleven o'clock as he usually did. By the time he finally did arrive, just before lunchtime, Nathan had accumulated a motley collection of vessels on his nightstand . . . a water glass, a Big Slurp plastic cup from the 7-Eleven, a Dr. Pepper bottle, an old flower pot he'd found on the shelf in the closet, and his regular returnable sample jar . . .all containing his urine. Dr. Smith walked in with a black eye and a puffy white bandage on his beaked nose. He looked disheveled, ruffled, like a flamingo who had been in a fight.

"What the hell happened to *you*?" Nathan asked.

Dr. Smith furtively shut the door and took a seat at Nathan's bedside. "I want to talk to you," he said earnestly.

"You been in a fight?"

"Yes. Not a fight, exactly. But someone hit me. I'll tell you about it later. Right now I want to ask you some questions."

Nathan was alarmed by Dr. Smith's serious tone. He felt the phantom throb, sharper now, in his rectum and remembered the chapter on cancer he'd read in *I'm Joe's Genitals*. With terror, he imagined that Dr. Smith was about to tell him his prostate was eaten up with malignancy.

"What do you do for a living?" Dr. Smith asked.

"What?"

"Lucinda said you are an artist. Can you make a living at that?"

"I sell copy machines. Why are you asking me this?"

"You're not a painter? . . . a sculptor?"

"I can't draw a straight line. I sell copy machines. I'm a salesman! What's this got to do with my . . . my condition?"

"Oh. Well. Then tell me, can you make good money selling copy machines?"

"What are you going to do? Give me a huge bill or something? What is this? Sock-it-to-me time?" Nathan was getting annoyed with Dr. Smith, but it wasn't the same irrational anger that he normally felt whenever he was around. For the first time, Nathan realized, the doctor was not mysteriously pissing him off.

"Please, just answer my questions," the doctor insisted.

"I get by," Nathan said. "I'll never get rich at it."

"Do you like being a salesman? Do you enjoy your work?"

"I despise it. What's it to you?"

Dr. Smith sat back in his chair and made a little church steeple with his fingers under his chin. "What would you say if I told you that you would never have to sell copy machines again? That you could walk out of here today and quit your groveling little job that you hate so passionately? What would you say, Nathan, if I told you that I can make you a rich man, that you will never have to work another day in your life?" Dr. Smith was beaming.

"I'd ask you if you were an Amway distributor." Nathan's tone was sarcastic, but he nevertheless felt a growing excitement, despite his skepticism.

"I'm serious, Nathan. What would you say?"

"Seriously, I'd ask you what's the catch."

"There's no catch, Nathan. What you would have to do to set yourself free for the rest of your life is so incredibly simple, natural, and easy, you won't believe it!"

"You're right. I probably won't. Now what's the catch?"

Dr. Smith squirmed in his chair. His hands were trembling, and he was sweating profusely. He gingerly touched the bandage on his nose and winced. He was stalling.

"What's the catch, Doctor?"

Dr. Smith cleared his throat. His Adam's apple rippled up and down his long, curved neck like a little animal struggling to escape from a tube sock.

"I will pay you $10,000 a month for your urine," he said flatly, averting his bloodshot eyes from Nathan's.

"What?" Nathan asked incredulously. "WHAT?"

"I need your urine, and I am prepared to pay you for it. Handsomely," Dr. Smith said, assuming a very businesslike tone of voice.

"What on earth could you possibly want with my piss?" Nathan asked. His excitement was building. Dr. Smith was, after all, a urologist, a scientist, a man who worked at one of the Southwest's leading teaching and medical research hospitals . . . a man whose very stock-in-trade was urine. What did *he* know?

"You're not going to believe this," Dr. Smith said. He was extremely nervous. He watched Nathan carefully.

"After what's happened to me in the past few days, nothing would surprise me, Doctor. Please. Go on."

"Your urine, Nathan, because of your recent accident, is testosterone-free. That makes it an extremely valuable commodity. To me."

"Why?"

"Because . . . because your urine still contains certain male hormones . . . and, more important, powerful pheromones . . . that are produced not in the testicles but in the hypothalamus, the pituitary gland, and the adrenal glands . . . and . . . and the point is . . . in *your* urine, Nathan, these pheromones are absolutely pure . . . uncontaminated by testosterone."

"Why is that important?" Nathan asked, now intensely interested.

"Because . . . because testosterone is counterproductive to the purpose for which I need your urine."

"Look," said Nathan impatiently. "Will you stop beating around the bush? What's this all about?"

Dr. Smith leaned forward, looking into Nathan's eyes, and took his hand between his now cold and clammy doctor hands.

"Can I trust you, Nathan? There's money in this for you, believe me! Can I *trust* you?"

"Yes," said Nathan. He withdrew his somehow de-flowered hand. "Lay it on me."

"Well," said Dr. Smith, "you've probably noticed a faint odor about me . . . a faint, but very disagreeable odor . . . an odor that has made you feel angry and aggressive toward me."

"Why, yes," said Nathan. "I have. But I'm not sure I necessarily made a connection . . . ."

"Precisely!" exclaimed Dr. Smith.

At that moment a nurse entered the room with Nathan's lunch on a tray.

"GET OUT!" shrieked Dr. Smith. The startled nurse dropped the tray on the floor.

"Well, exCUSE ME!" she retorted. She backed quickly out of the room and slammed the door.

"Forgive me," Dr. Smith said to Nathan, "but this is *extremely* confidential, what I'm telling you now."

"You can trust me," Nathan said, fascinated.

"Good. Now. Let me ask you this: How do you feel toward me today? Do you still feel angry? Aggressive?"

"No. Actually I don't. Not today."

"Precisely!"

"Precisely?"

"Yes! Because, you see, Nathan, *today* I am wearing *your* urine!"

"YOU'RE WHAT?"

"Every other day I've worn *ordinary* urine contaminated with testosterone! Don't you see?"

"No! I don't fucking see! What the fuck are you talking about?"

"Nathan, Nathan! The pheromones in the testosterone were what made you so angry!"

"SO?!!!"

"So that means that if I make *Pierre: For Men* with *your* urine I can still attract women like flies *without* the dangerous side effects produced by testosterone! Isn't that fanTASTIC?"

"That's fantastic, all right," said Nathan, beginning to understand. "*Pierre: For Men* . . . that's your aftershave, isn't it?"

"Cologne, actually. For men. It's a subtle blend of male urine and about a dozen secret herbs and spices. It's the most powerful aphrodisiac ever known to man!" Dr. Smith said proudly. "After eight tedious, frustrating years of research and experimentation, I have finally hit upon the magic combination! Thanks to you, Nathan."

"Tell me about your black eye," said Nathan. "And your nose."

"Oh, that!" laughed Dr. Smith, lightly touching his bandaged beak. "I'll never have *that* problem again. You see, all the time I've been experimenting with *ordinary* urine, I've had to beat the women off with a stick, all right, but I've also had to run for my life more than once from irrationally aggressive men. That's always been the big fly in the ointment. So last night I decided to make up a batch of

Pierre: For Men with *your* urine, which I've been analyzing all week. I splashed some on and went out on the town. And let me tell you, Nathan, it was like night and day! The women were *still* all over me, but for the first time ever, the men *ignored* me!"

"But what about your face?" Nathan persisted.

"I was coming to that," said Dr. Smith, gently touching his nose again. "This is the result of my acid test, so to speak . . . the scientific, empirical proof of the success of my new formula . . . *our* formula, Nathan. After achieving such incredible results with *your* urine, I decided when I got home last night to switch back to *ordinary* urine one more time . . . just to make sure . . . and went out again. I suppose I had become lulled into a false sense of safety, for I failed to react quickly enough when a man suddenly and viciously attacked me in a singles bar at about two a.m. this morning."

"I see," said Nathan, impressed.

"It *works*, Nathan. It really *works*!" said Dr. Smith radiantly. "I can make a fortune off this! And I can set you free, at last! Are you *with* me, Boy?"

"I guess every cloud has a silver lining," said Nathan. "A dog bites off my only nut, and I suddenly come into a fortune. It's almost Dickensian."

"Well, not exactly a fortune, Nathan. I'll pay you, as I said, $10,000 a month for your urine. The raw material. Don't forget, I'll have to bear the heavy expense of start-up costs, machinery, manufacturing, packaging, marketing, TV advertising. My pay-off will come in the long haul."

"O.K. Let's see, then. At $10,000 a month, you already owe me $2,500 for the past week's piss," Nathan said, testing Dr. Smith's sincerity. He indicated with a sweep of his hand the array of urine-filled vessels on the nightstand.

"No problem," said Dr. Smith, reaching into his coat pocket. He pulled out his checkbook and a pen. "Here's a check for $12,500," he said, writing briskly. "$2,500 for services rendered to date, and $10,000 for the first month in advance." He handed Nathan the check.

"Gosh," said Nathan. It was more money than he'd ever had at one time in his life.

"No problem," said Dr. Smith again. "I'm *already* a wealthy man. I *am* a doctor, you know."

"Gosh," said Nathan again, still looking at the check. "How do I . . . I mean . . . what do I have to do? Just piss in a bottle every day and give it to you?"

"That's basically it," said Dr. Smith. "I'll call you tomorrow with details, after I set up a meeting with my lawyer, you, and myself."

"Lawyer?" Nathan's blood turned cold. The only advice he could remember his father ever giving him was: "Nathan, whatever you wind up doing in this goofy world, avoid lawyers at all costs." Nathan's life experiences to date had borne out the wisdom of that caveat.

"What do we need a lawyer for?" Nathan asked pleadingly.

"Well, it all has to be legal," Dr. Smith said. "Contracts, non-disclosure agreement . . . all that sort of thing. It's standard business procedure. Routine. Nothing to worry about. All you will be required to do is urinate copiously and collect your check every month." He smiled with genuine affection and clapped his clean, well-manicured doctor/business tycoon hand on Nathan's shoulder.

"O.K . . . I guess," Nathan responded weakly. His head was swimming, and he felt the sharpening pain in his rectum inching downward toward his anus. He clutched the check in his hand. "You'll . . . you'll call me?"

"Tomorrow," said Dr. Smith. "Oh, and by the way, Nathan, I'm sure you realize that testosterone shots are out . . . under the circumstances."

"What?"

"Testosterone therapy. That's no longer indicated as a clinical treatment option for your . . . condition."

"But . . . but . . . ."

"It's nothing to worry about, Nathan. You'll be just fine. You know, you really *are* a very lucky man to be totally free of testosterone. Testosterone only spells trouble, believe me."

"But . . . but . . . what about my sex drive? I'll lose my libido. I've been reading about it!"

"Trust me, Nathan. I don't think you'll miss a thing. It's a minor trade-off. Think about all the money and freedom you'll have! Trust me! You won't miss it!"

"But . . . but . . . my body! I'll become pear-shaped! I read about it! My ass will get fat! I'll lose my body hair!"

"Nathan, Nathan! You're almost fifty years old! What do you care about body hair? Live! For once in your miserable, poverty-stricken life, LIVE! Enjoy! Be free!"

"But . . . ."

"Look, Goddammit! What do you want? Pussy or freedom? Make up your mind!"

Nathan considered the choice. It was pretty black and white. Dr. Smith stared at him, silent, motionless. Nathan saw that he was too good a businessman to blink first. He thought about never having intercourse again, and that gave him a pang of regret. Then he thought about his first love . . . cunnilingus. That would still be possible, of course, as long as he had the desire to engage in it. And that was all most women he'd known really wanted anyway . . . after they discovered his special talent. He thought about what Lucinda had said so sincerely the night she gave him that glorious tongue bath: "It makes me happy just to lick you . . . any way you are . . . and to have you lick me."

Nathan looked at Dr. Smith and blinked.

"Freedom," he said.

FIVE

Lucinda arrived at the hospital at one o'clock in the afternoon, barely thirty minutes after Nathan had made his fateful decision to accept freedom from Dr. Peter Smith. She had come to take him home with her to La Coterie, to begin his convalescence, to nurse him back to emotional and spiritual wholeness. She felt happy, excited, motherly.

When she walked into the room, Nathan was lying in bed, his eyes riveted to the television set hung high on the opposite wall. He was watching, and listening, in slack-jawed astonishment.

"Kashanda! Boh-tanda!" intoned the impassioned man on the screen. "Quo-dah-bah-sah-tah! Doh-boh-duh-soy-yuh!" It was Brother Larry Proffitt, the evangelical miracle-maker of Faith 'N Fortune Television Ministries. He was speaking in tongues.

"Satan!" he shouted, banging his tiny pink fist on his Bible, "you evil spirit of infirmity! Come OUT of that liver! In the name of GEE-zus! I COMMAND you!" He slammed his fist again on his Bible, and his diamond-clustered ring and heavy gold identification bracelet sparkled in the bright television studio lights. So did his snake-like eyes and his fastidiously combed and oiled pompadour.

"Hey, Sport!" Lucinda called out cheerfully. "Ready to get out of this place?"

"Wait a minute, Lucinda," Nathan said, still looking at the television in amazement. "Look at this! Will you *look* at this guy? Who the hell *is* this idiot?" Nathan never watched TV. He was unaware of much of the lunacy broadcast on the fringe channels.

"Oh, that's Larry Proffitt," Lucinda said. "Haven't you ever seen his show before? He's incredible! An absolute nut! He's one of my best customers."

"Customers?"

"Yes. He's filthy rich."

"What does he buy? Madonna-with-child paintings?"

"Actually, his tastes lean more toward erotic sculpture. He's bought at least a dozen works from my gallery over the last two years."

"But . . . he preaches *against* pornography! I've been watching! That's his main thing!"

"I do not sell pornographic art in my gallery, Nathan," Lucinda said indignantly.

"But, I mean his whole *focus* is anti-sex!"

It was true. Like most televangelical zealots, Larry Proffitt was obsessed with a particular aspect of evil. His passion was not the evil of communism. Nor was it the evil of Judaism, nor Catholicism, nor secular humanism, nor alcoholism, nor any other ism. Brother Proffitt's divine focus was the evil of "perversion, pornography, and fornication," which he sometimes inadvertently pronounced "perversion, fornography, and pornication." He had a large and diverse audience of diseased, terrified, guilt-ridden sinners eager to repent.

Luckily, according to Brother Larry, securing God's forgiveness was a piece of cake: Simply plant a $1,000 "seed of faith" in the fertile Faith 'N Fortune bank account, and Jesus would absolve you of all your past sexual abominations, and make you rich, to boot. Not only that, He would also miraculously heal your gonorrhea, your venereal warts, your herpes infection, and even your failing liver, as he was doing now.

"Get OUT of that liver, Satan! In the name of GEE-zus I BANISH thee to eternal HELL and DAMNATION! Oh, yes, Lord! Your spirit is ah-PONE me! Kashanda! Boh-tanda! Ree-doo-koo! Quo-dah-bah-sah-tah!"

Brother Larry, a former used car salesman and frequenter of Dallas' many topless clubs for gentlemen, had been born again. But he had not lost his knack for salesmanship, his instinct for what turned people on and what turned them off. He knew, for example, that when speaking in tongues on television, one should speak only in "media tongue bites." He understood that an entire cryptic, babbling paragraph or even a complete sentence in tongues would never fly on TV, where the attention span of his average viewer rarely exceeded three nanoseconds unless he was pandering with clear, bright, colorful images to the reptilian root of their brain.

"Doh-boh-duh-soy-yuh!" said Larry Proffitt. The camera zoomed in to a close-up of his contorted face so that all the dim-witted pornicators in TV-land could see his little snake eyes filling with tears. "Oh, thank you, Jesus," he said, his lips and chin trembling with emotion. He shut his eyes tightly, forcing a tear to trickle down his pink cheek.

"What an *incredible* performance!" Nathan exclaimed. "He ought to be selling copy machines! He'd make millions!"

Lucinda switched off the TV. "He already does, believe me," she said. "Let's get out of here."

Lucinda had planned a special discharge celebration meal for Nathan to make up for a week's worth of lousy hospital food. She drove her turbo Saab toward North Dallas to her favorite up-scale, power-lunch restaurant, a little Italian theme cafe that specialized in expensive, trendy pasta dishes. Nathan knew the spot.

The restaurant, a Dallas landmark since 1936 (and therefore on the Dallas Historical Society's list of historic buildings), had originally opened as a barbecue joint and had done a good business for nearly half a century. Nathan loved Texas barbecue and had eaten there often. But when sushi became the "in" food several years back, the descendants of the restaurant's founder suddenly switched cuisine and transmogrified the dusty, Old West atmosphere into a slick, minimalist Japanese ambiance. They did well, doubling their profits, until a software salesman nearly died from an intestinal worm infestation and closed them down. After winning the nasty, ensuing lawsuit, they reopened as the "Pasta Emporium," just in time for the new American romance with cholesterol-free food.

After six months of unprecedented earnings, they went public and opened a chain of franchised Pasta Emporiums all across the United States. But this was not unusual; Dallas had spawned more theme restaurant franchise operations than any other city in the country. If there was one thing Dallasites liked to do, thought Nathan, it was to eat out. There really wasn't much else to do.

On the way to the restaurant, Nathan asked Lucinda to stop at his bank. He went in alone and deposited Dr. Smith's check in his account. He hoped it would clear before his meeting with the lawyer.

Nathan had decided not to tell Lucinda about his deal with Dr. Smith. He didn't really know her that well, yet, and was afraid she might find the whole business disgusting, or worse, unethical. Nathan wasn't sure how he felt about it himself. He wanted time to think about it, though he knew he had pretty much made up his mind. Freedom was hard to come by this day and time.

Lucinda wheeled into the crowded Pasta Emporium parking lot. As she pulled into an empty space, Nathan noticed an unusual license plate on a brand new BMW parked in front of them. "I SUE

4 U," it said.

"Fucking lawyer," Nathan hissed under his breath.

"What?" Lucinda asked.

"Nothing. I was just noticing that car ahead of us. Look at that stupid license plate!" he said as they got out of Lucinda's Saab.

Lucinda looked. "Oh, cute!" she said appreciatively. "Must belong to an attorney."

"Yeah. Look at all those aerials," said Nathan, smirking. There were four antennas sprouting from the car: radio, CB, cellular phone, and (though Nathan did not recognize it) police radio. "Looks like a goddamned communications satellite," he sneered. He then went into a silly, sarcastic, mocking routine that Lucinda found exceedingly obnoxious. "Oh dear! Oh dear me!" Nathan simpered. "This car must belong to a *very* important, *busy* attorney-at-law! Oh dear! I wonder if we should even *presume* to eat in the same trendy, yuppie restaurant with such a *terribly important, busy, busy* man!"

"What's the *matter* with you?" Lucinda snapped. She looked around to see if anyone else had heard him. "Have you lost your mind? You're acting like a twit!"

"Come on," Nathan said, his face reddening with embarrassment. He took Lucinda's hand and headed for the restaurant door.

"Do you have something against lawyers?" Lucinda whispered as she followed him. She wanted an explanation for his strange and completely unexpected outburst.

"Yes," said Nathan. "I'm sorry. I'll tell you about it sometime."

The Pasta Emporium hostess, dressed in a pink and white checked pinafore and a pink puffed up chef's cap, seated them and took their drink order.

"Well?" Lucinda asked Nathan. She was curious about his obvious animosity toward the legal profession. She was determined to get an answer.

"Well, what?"

"Tell me why you hate lawyers."

"It . . . it happened a long time ago. I . . . ." Nathan looked around behind him at the adjacent table. Three young men in business suits were talking and laughing loudly, annoying him. He contained his rising anger, and turned back to Lucinda. "I . . . ."

At that moment, a telephone rang. At the adjacent table. The man nearest Nathan whipped a small cellular phone from a leather holster on his belt.

"Skinner, Wilson, and Goldfarb," he announced into the mouthpiece. "Yes . . . . Yes . . . . This is J. Charleton Skinner, III, speaking . . . . Yes . . . . Oh, really? What channel?" He cupped his hand over the mouthpiece. "He saw our ad on TV!" he said to the other two men, presumably Wilson and Goldfarb. They all smiled conspiratorially at each other. "Yes . . . . I see . . . . Yes . . . . Yes . . . . Did you run into him, or did he hit you? . . . . Good! . . . . I see . . . . Yes . . . . Yes, Mr. Davis, I can *certainly* help you! I'm glad you called. Now, listen to me. Do not discuss your accident with anyone! I'm in conference with another client at the moment, but I'll be at the hospital within one hour. What is your room number? Good. Hang in there, Mr. Davis. You're about to become a wealthy man. See you in an hour! Good-bye!" He switched off the phone.

"Bingo!" he said.

J. Charleton Skinner, III, returned the phone to his holster with a flourish and looked at his cohorts with a poker face.

"That, gentlemen, was Mr. Benjamin P. Davis," he said, barely containing his glee. Wilson and Goldfarb were on the edges of their Pasta Emporium bentwood chairs.

"And . . . ?" they asked in unison, their eyes glistening with avarice.

"It seems Mr. Davis is in a body cast at Parkland Memorial Hospital. He is suffering greatly from two broken legs and a fractured spine, which will no doubt never properly heal."

"No doubt," chimed in Wilson and Goldfarb.

"Last night, while riding his motorcycle home from work, he was struck by a speeding beer truck. The driver of said beer truck is now incarcerated in the Lew Sterrett Justice Center on charges of reckless driving and leaving the scene of an accident."

As if on cue, the trio of senior partners in the sleazeball law firm of Skinner, Wilson, and Goldfarb, P.C., burst into song.

"We're in the mon-ey!" they sang. "We're in the mon-ey!" They slapped the table and reared back in their flimsy chairs, laughing raucously.

"Excuse me!" Nathan said to J. Charleton Skinner, III. "Would you please hold it down?"

The singing and laughing stopped abruptly. Skinner turned in his chair and looked at Nathan. He looked him up and down, slowly, from head to toe.

"You're not from around here, are you, Boy?" Skinner seemed to be making an observation rather than asking a question. Nathan noticed that he wore a heavy gold and diamond ring on his left hand, and a Southern Methodist University ring on his right hand.

"No, I'm from Virginia," Nathan said. "But I live here now, and you are disturbing me and my friend."

"Well," drawled Skinner, his voice dripping with contempt, "it's *obvious* you're not a *native* Texan."

"No, thankfully, I'm not," said Nathan. "However, I have lived in this wasteland you call a state for twenty years, and it has been like infinity in hell for me."

Lucinda gasped. She clutched Nathan's arm. "Let's go!" she

begged. But Skinner suddenly stood up, towering over Nathan, and threateningly removed his expensive suit jacket. He was wearing red suspenders, or "braces," as the designers call them these days; they had little ducks imprinted on them. He was also wearing Texas-chic Tony Lama cowboy boots made from the hides of several unfortunate armadillos.

"Well, I'd shore like to help you go back to Ol' Virginny," said Skinner. "It would be mighty good riddance!"

"Go fuck yourself," Nathan said calmly. Lucinda gasped again.

"Pardon me?" said Skinner, removing his Submariner Rolex watch and placing it on the table. He seemed scarcely able to believe his ears.

"No, pardon *me*," said Nathan, standing up and clumsily knocking over his chair. "Let me see if I can put it in a more Latinate vernacular . . . terms that a brilliant legal mind such as yours might better comprehend: Go invaginate your own posterior orifice with your own pudendum!"

"Why, you're a real smartass, aren't you, Boy?" Skinner said, puffing himself up. "I ought to kick your ass from here to Corpus Christi!"

Nathan drew back his clenched fist. "You so much as touch me and I'll break your fucking neck!"

Nathan called a good bluff. He was about the same size as Skinner, and he was obviously physically fit. But what was truly intimidating about him was his air of total self-confidence. This was a manifestation of his lifelong, self-destructive delusion, when angry, that he was bulletproof, a delusion that accounted for most of his bouts with unconsciousness as a teenager.

Skinner backed down. He put his coat back on and, letting good business sense be the better part of valor, said, "You hit me and I'll sue your smartass for all you're worth!"

Nathan was thinking about hitting him anyway, when he was suddenly gripped by an excruciating pain in his anus. The pain was so intense and relentless that he became nauseated, then dizzy, and finally fainted, demolishing the spindly Pasta Emporium table as he fell.

When Nathan came around several minutes later, Lucinda was sitting on the rubble of the broken table, holding his head in her lap. The alarmed hostess had brought ice, twisted in a pink and white checked Pasta Emporium linen napkin, and Lucinda was holding it to Nathan's forehead with one hand and fanning his face with her other. A crowd of diners had left their little tables and were gathered around them, gawking.

To Nathan's great relief, the pain had subsided to a still sharp, but gradually decreasing, throb that seemed to move in a slow circle, round and round his anus.

"Where's that son of a bitch?" Nathan asked feverishly. Skinner and his cronies had left immediately, fearing a possible lawsuit. They were all piled in the BMW, radios crackling, speeding toward Parkland Memorial Hospital.

"Calm down, Nathan. He's gone," said Lucinda soothingly. "I'm taking you home."

"If I ever see that motherfucker again, I'll . . . I'll . . . ."

"Nathan! Hush!"

"Did you hear the way he talked to me? That sleazy, goddamn . . . ."

"Yes, Nathan. He had no right to speak to you that way," said Lucinda. "Come on now, let's go." She helped him to his feet.

As they walked out to the car, Lucinda reflected that while she, herself, had found Skinner's behavior and manner unforgivably rude and coarse, she nevertheless had found him curiously attractive. As he had hurriedly passed her on his way out of the restaurant, she had caught a whiff of his aftershave . . . or cologne. If she was not mistaken, he was wearing *Pierre: For Men*.

SIX

On the way to La Coterie, Nathan told Lucinda all about his ex-wife Nancy. And about Rose, his long lost daughter. And he told her about Jimmy McCracken, his high school nemesis and legal adversary during his divorce.

He told her about how he had vied with McCracken for three years in school for Nancy's affections, about how McCracken had been the most popular boy in school: football hero, class president, member of the Key Club, an officer in the Honor Society, senior class valedictorian. "He could have had any other girl in the school he wanted," Nathan said, "but he wanted Nancy." Nancy had dated both of them, making them bitter enemies. McCracken had once knocked Nathan cold with a single punch at a basketball game in front of a bleacherful of classmates. Most of the students had cheered.

Nathan had been an outsider, morose, non-participatory. He had lacked school spirit. His manic depression had been misdiagnosed. He was considered a troublemaker, a maverick, a borderline juvenile delinquent. He'd dropped out of school in the middle of his senior year and had gone to work selling Fuller Brushes door-to-door.

McCracken, whose impassioned valedictory address on the American Dream had been published in the *Richmond Times Dispatch*, had gone on to study law at the University of Virginia. Nancy stayed behind and eventually married Nathan, who was doing well selling Fuller Brushes, well enough to buy a brand new Mustang convertible. They were only nineteen years old.

After several years of blissful marriage, Rose was born. On Rose's second birthday, Jimmy McCracken was graduated from law school at the top of his class and was tapped by Richmond's largest and most prestigious law firm. That's when the trouble started.

Nathan, still plagued by the alternating darkness and blinding lights of manic depression, sensed he was slowly, ineluctably, losing the love and respect of his young wife. He became more and more erratic in his behavior. One evening after dinner, Nancy showed him an article from the *Times Dispatch* "Personalities" section. It was all about Jimmy McCracken and his brilliant legal career. "He called me today," she said proudly, nostalgically. "Just to say 'Hi.'"

Nathan flew into a rage, lost control. He stormed out of their apartment, jumped into his Mustang, and peeled out, only to run a red light and slam broadside into a police cruiser. He verbally abused the cops, resisted arrest, and was finally hauled off to the Medical College of Virginia psycho ward, babbling incoherently about the "hubris," "mendacity," and "venality" of lawyers, doctors, and bankers. The cops thought he was speaking in tongues.

He was released in less than a week, but it was too late. Nancy had already filed for divorce. And she had retained Jimmy McCracken as her attorney.

It was a bitter and hard-fought year-long divorce proceeding. Unfortunately, Nathan was in a manic phase when the final hearing rolled around, and he unwisely chose to defend himself in court, thumbing his nose at the value of legal representation. McCracken crucified him. Nathan lost his temper in front of the judge and was found in contempt of court. He lost everything, including the right to ever see his daughter again.

Two weeks after the final decree, Nancy married McCracken. On their wedding night, Nathan broke into the McCracken home, trying to find Rose. McCracken decked him again, in front of his daughter. "You're a loser, Doering," he'd said. "You've always been a loser, and you always will be. Now get out of my house, or I'll have you committed for life." Nathan had left, believing him. It was the last time he ever saw Rose.

The next day, still a young man, he took an Indiana newspaperman's advice, left the verdant hills and peaceful valleys of Virginia, and went west . . . to a glittering apparition on the vast, barren prairie . . . to the mirage of an improbable city hovering inexplicably on the blazingly hot, desolate plains of Texas . . . to Big D, little a, double l, a, s.

Lucinda pulled up to the heavy iron gate blocking the driveway into La Coterie. She activated the special infrared "key" mounted on her dashboard, and the gate swung open with a rusty, scraping sound. They drove into the gingerbread compound, like Hansel and Gretel, and the gate closed ominously behind them. Lucinda wended her way through the narrow lanes and turned into the carport behind her condo. The carport was fringed in gingerbread, too. Nathan's Toyota hatchback was already parked there. Lucinda had fetched it from where he had parked it near her gallery the day he and Baby Bow Wow had tangled.

When Nathan stepped out of the Saab, the first thing he noticed, or rather heard, was dogs. Barking dogs. Apparently dozens of them, from all directions. A shiver went up his spine. He wondered if Baby Bow Wow was out there among them. He had recently read an article in *Smithsonian* magazine about an exhaustive scientific investigation into why dogs bark. They bark, the researchers had finally concluded after years of study, "just for the hell of it."

"Christ! It sounds like a fucking kennel in here!" Nathan said.

"You know, Nathan, I really wish you would watch your language. Every other word is either an obscenity or a profanity."

"I'm sorry," he said. "It's a bad habit. I'll try to work on it."

"Thank you."

"What's with all the fucking dogs?"

"You'll have to work harder than that!"

"O.K. What's with all the . . . dogs?"

"Just about everyone here has one," Lucinda said. "It's gotten a little out of hand. Sometimes the noise is unbearable. The barking actually keeps me awake some nights."

"Oh, that's just great!" said Nathan. He had no use for dogs, especially since his encounter with Baby Bow Wow. He had never understood his countrymen's mania for pets, anyway. Especially their sappy affection for dogs and cats. "What about cats?" he asked.

"No cats," Lucinda said. "There used to be two or three. The last one had a nervous breakdown and lost all its fur. At least that's what Pops told me."

"Who's Pops?"

"He's the gatekeeper. You'll meet him when you get your ID number and infrared key so you can get in and out by yourself."

Lucinda unlocked the back door to her condo and stepped into the kitchen. Baby Bow Wow instantly skittered in from the dining room and glommed onto her leg, humping away.

"Baby Bow Wow! NO!" shouted Lucinda, pushing him down. "God, I *hate* it when he does that!"

"He evidently does that every time he sees you," Nathan said.

Lucinda stooped and took the dog's little pug-nosed snout in her hand. "Baby Bow Wow, Nathan is coming to stay with us. Now you be nice to him, you hear?"

"Grrrrr," growled Baby Bow Wow, twisting free of Lucinda's hand

and baring his sharp little teeth. He lowered his head, snarling at Nathan, and thrust each hind leg back stiffly in a macho demonstration of his intent to protect his territory. Instead of kicking up dust like the brute in the wild he imagined himself to be, he laid down little scratches on Lucinda's polished parquet kitchen floor with his tiny claws.

The hairs on the back of Nathan's neck stood up. Staring back hard at the dog, he asked Lucinda, "What on earth possessed you to name this nasty, evil little rodent Baby Bow Wow?"

"Now listen, you two!" Lucinda scolded with mock impatience. "I won't have any more of your silly fighting in this house! You be *sweet* to each other!" She was trying to ease the tension. It didn't work.

Nathan growled at Baby Bow Wow, taunting him. Baby Bow Wow tried to charge at Nathan but merely spun his wheels, so to speak, on the slick floor. He inched forward in a blur of tiny, muscular legs, snarling and snapping, leaving hundreds of little scratches in his wake. Nathan watched the infuriated, hysterical terrier moving slowly toward him and imagined what super-canine acceleration this dog could achieve with a proper purchase. As Baby Bow Wow gained momentum, Nathan instinctively moved to the kitchen counter, opened a drawer, and pulled out a butcher knife.

"NATHAN! NO!" Lucinda screamed.

Lucinda's scream was so loud, louder even than the sexual scream she had let loose the day they had met, that both Nathan and Baby Bow Wow stopped dead in their tracks. Nathan dropped the knife on the floor, and Baby Bow Wow ducked through the little hinged panel in the kitchen door and disappeared, melting into the pack of some hundred-odd other dogs roving La Coterie Arts District Living Centre.

53

Lucinda took Nathan into the living room, sat him down on the Early American sofa, and poured him a drink . . . a strange mixture of Dr. Pepper and Mexican tequila.

"If you're going to live with me, you're going to have to get along with my dog," she said.

"Is that an ultimatum?"

"Yes, if that's what you want to call it."

"How can you think of keeping that mutt after what he did to me?"

"Nathan, he's just a dog, for Christ's sake! You can't blame a stupid animal for being a stupid animal. You can't just kill him for doing what comes naturally to him!"

"If castrating your lovers is what comes naturally to him, I'd say you've got a serious problem on your hands!"

"You were going to kill him with that knife, weren't you?"

"No. Really, I wasn't. I don't know what came over me. Look, couldn't you just give him away? Maybe you could give him to one of your customers. Maybe you could even *sell* him to Brother Larry Proffitt as erotic dog art. The little beast always has a hard-on!"

"That's not funny, Nathan!" Nathan was learning that Lucinda was sensitive about her art gallery. "Giving Baby Bow Wow away is out of the question," she said. "He was a . . . a gift."

"Gift? Did you know that the word 'gift' in the German language means 'poison'?" Nathan, though a high school drop-out, had read widely but not deeply. He had therefore achieved a spotty and highly eclectic self-education.

"No. I did not know that."

"Well, tell me, what misguided or hateful fool bestowed the great *gift* of Baby Bow Wow upon you?"

"An artist friend of mine . . . Boris Bronowsky," Lucinda said, thinking back dreamily. She took a sip of her tequila and Dr. Pepper highball. "He was a genius. Unfortunately, he's dead now. But, oh . . . when he was alive! What fabulous art he produced! He worked in plastic and neon. He created fantastic representations of religious icons: the crucifix, the Star of David, the swastika, the madonna, the Menorah. You name it! Then he moved into religious abstractions. Heaven. Hell. Purgatory. Oh, he was good, Nathan. He was *so* good! His most ambitious work, and sadly his last, was a powerful and terrifying representation of the Holy Ghost."

She put her drink down, closed her eyes, and massaged her temples with her fingertips.

"But, alas, Boris, like so many other great artists in history, became personally ensnarled in the perceived significance of his own work."

Boris had, in fact, lost touch with reality while working on the Holy Ghost piece. He went to India, Lucinda told Nathan, mucked around in the mountains with bald-headed monks for awhile, came back to Dallas, became a vegetarian, and was briefly hospitalized at Parkland for malnutrition as a consequence. In this weakened state he had had a vision while watching Faith 'N Fortune on television. He immediately called the number on the screen and pledged to Brother Larry Proffitt all of his work as a "seed of faith" . . . all of his work, that is, that Lucinda had not already sold at exorbitant prices through her gallery or bought for herself as an investment.

After being discharged from Parkland, Boris began attending live worship services on Sunday mornings and Wednesday nights at Proffitt's subsidiary Faith World Pentecostal Church On The Rock (which was actually a remodeled pre-fab warehouse on a concrete slab previously owned by the bankrupt car dealership where Brother Larry had worked before he was born again). Boris soon became convinced that the Rapture was imminent. At high noon on a workday in downtown Dallas, Boris Bronowsky climbed to the roof of the Texas Bank and Trust Company building and performed what an accountant on his lunch break called a "swan dive." The accountant had been quoted in the *Dallas Morning News* as an eyewitness.

"Actually," Lucinda said, "I don't think he jumped. I think he lost his balance in the terrible wind that whips around those skyscrapers and fell. He radiated such joy in his last few days. He was certain that the Rapture was coming, and I think he climbed to that rooftop simply because he wanted to be first up."

"That's a very sad story," Nathan said. The tequila was starting to make his nose go numb.

"Anyway, he was a sap," Lucinda said, freshening her drink. "He went out and bought me this goddamn puppy as some kind of mawkish love-gift. What could I say, Nathan? What could I *do*? If I'd told him I didn't want the damned thing it would have crushed him."

"I know. I know."

"I mean Boris was *so excited* because this dog . . . this is *so incredible*, Nathan . . . this puppy, every time it barked it made a sound like someone trying to say 'Yahweh' while clearing their throat! I'm *serious*!"

Lucinda began to get the giggles.

"What?"

"Yahweh!" Lucinda barked while violently clearing her throat. Then she cracked up. Nathan began to giggle. It was strong tequila.

"What does 'Yahweh' mean?" asked Nathan.

"Yahweh, the ancient, sacred, secret name of God. Haven't you heard of it?"

"No, I guess not." Nathan was embarrassed at the revelation of yet another of the many gaps in his self-education. He had already exposed his ignorance during one of their long conversations at the hospital. He had not known the difference between a modernist and a post-modernist.

"Well, anyway," giggled Lucinda, "Boris found it highly significant that a dog . . . which is God spelled backwards, by the way, as Boris was constantly pointing out . . . he found it highly significant that a dog would continually pronounce the ancient name of God for no apparent reason." Lucinda was now almost out of control with knee-slapping mirth. "So . . . so he named the dog Yahweh!" she wheezed.

"I thought his name was Baby Bow Wow," Nathan said. He was confused and a bit tipsy.

"Oh, that came later. Boris fell in love with that dog, I *swear*. He cuddled it all the time . . . he even kissed it on the *mouth*, Nathan! And he talked *baby* talk to it: 'Does my widdle baby bow wow wanna bone? Does him?'" Lucinda did her Boris imitation without mercy. "He even *slept* with him, Nathan! It was always Baby this and Baby that till I thought I would throw up. Anyway, it finally became Baby Bow Wow. That's what we wound up calling him."

"Did Boris live with you, Lucinda?"

"Yes. He did. Does that bother you?"

"No," Nathan lied.

"YAHWEH!" barked Baby Bow Wow from the kitchen.

He had returned, and He wanted His dinner.

SEVEN

Nathan and Lucinda had fallen into the waterbed with their clothes on, too drunk on tequila to consummate their new living arrangement. During the night, Nathan woke up groggily, needing to go to the bathroom. In a stupor, but as if programmed by Dr. Smith to perform his new duty, he bypassed the bathroom, went downstairs to his briefcase, opened it, and removed one of the eight large, sterilized, urine sample jars the doctor had given him the day before. He removed the twist-on cap and emptied his bladder. He replaced the now warm and golden jar in his briefcase, snapped it shut, and spun the combination lock. He went back upstairs and went back to bed, still fully clothed.

The next morning, Nathan took a shower under Lucinda's high-tech Massage-O-Matic showerhead. He shaved and dressed, putting on the new, white, one hundred percent cotton Polo shirt that Lucinda had bought and laid out for him on the waterbed. He went downstairs and joined her in the kitchen for breakfast.

"Good morning!" Lucinda said brightly. "Good-looking shirt."

"Thanks," said Nathan. He kissed her. "Where's Baby Bow Wow?" he asked, looking around cautiously.

"He's out."

"Good. Where's my testicle, Lucinda?"

"It's in the freezer. I didn't know what to do with it."

"Thanks," said Nathan.

"What *are* you going to do with it?"

"I don't know yet." Nathan thoughtfully took a bite of toast.

"Well, I have a big day today," Lucinda said. "I've discovered a new artist, Nathan. A true genius. He's coming by to discuss a major one-man show at the gallery."

"Who is it?"

"His name is Vincent D'Amato. He's been living in obscurity in an East Dallas garage for fifteen years working like a madman. I can't *believe* my good fortune! This guy could be the biggest find of my career. Believe me, Nathan, Vincent's going to take Dallas by storm when his show opens. He could go all the way. New York. Paris! He's an *unbelievable* genius!"

"What is he, a painter?"

"He's everything! The world is his medium! He can create incredible art out of virtually anything. And he does! Do you know what he said to me?"

"No."

"He said that just being alive is a performance art! Isn't that beautiful? I mean everything this guy does is art! He lives, breathes, eats, and sleeps art! I've never seen such commitment. Such *involvement!*"

"Sounds a bit tedious to me."

"No, no, Nathan. You don't understand. I mean he finds joy, pure artistic joy, in the simplest, most mundane acts. While I was at his studio looking at all the simply *incredible* things he's created, he actually sat down on the floor and put on his socks! 'Look!' he said to me, 'Man Putting On Socks!' Now *that's* artistic *involvement!*"

"Sounds like a nut to me," Nathan said, finishing his orange juice. He felt a sudden, uncomfortable surge of jealousy. Why had D'Amato been barefooted in the first place? Had he been bare-assed as well? Had he and Lucinda been having "performance-art" sex in his sordid little garage studio? Nathan fought to suppress his rising sense of insecurity. What do I care? he thought. I'm only living here temporarily. There's no commitment. She's never told me she loves me. I don't own her.

"Well, I have a big day planned, too," Nathan said.

"Going back to work?"

"No, actually I thought I would take a leave of absence for a while," he lied. "I haven't had a vacation in years. Thought I might take some time to re-think my priorities. I've got some money set aside." Right, Nathan thought excitedly. $12,500 at the moment, and more, much more to come. "I've got some errands to run, some business to take care of. And I need to run by my house and pick up some things. My clothes. And some books. You don't mind if I bring my books, do you?"

"Of course not, Nathan. You bring anything you want." Lucinda kissed him on the mouth and took his face in her hands. "I'm really glad you're here," she said, looking into his eyes, smiling.

Nathan suddenly felt better about D'Amato.

Lucinda took Nathan out to meet Pops MacDonald, the compound gatekeeper. He was a jolly, rotund man in his seventies, semi-retired and widowed. He lived at La Coterie, too. Nathan liked him, and it seemed to be mutual. Pops gave Nathan a security code number for the walk-in gate and an infrared "key" for the driveway gate. "Glad to have you as a neighbor, Son," he said kindly, and then he winked knowingly at Nathan. Nathan winked back, then wished he hadn't. "Come by and visit sometime," Pops said. "I'll tell you all about the interesting history of La Coterie."

Lucinda gave Nathan keys to her condo, kissed him passionately, and then they parted to go their separate ways for the day.

Nathan's first stop was the bank. He had dealt there for years, had sold them four large copy machines, and he knew the management staff well. He asked the head cashier, as a personal favor, to verify and clear the check he had deposited the day before. She did; the check was good, and Nathan withdrew $1,000.

Next, he stopped by a chemical supply house and bought a quart of formaldehyde.

And then he walked into Acme Business Machines to quit his job.

Jerry Frick, the sales manager, had the entire sales force in the "war room," a little antechamber off the demo area, undergoing their weekly mass hypnosis. From outside, Nathan could hear the familiar basso profundo voice of the hypnotist: "Deeper and deeper . . . you're going deeper and deee-per and deeeee-per into a peaceful sleeeeeeep."

Frick had a friend named Van Hoosier who was a part-time handwriting analyst and self-taught hypnotist. He looked a lot like Raymond Burr, and he had helped Frick stop smoking. Frick was so impressed with his talents that he now not only required every new applicant for a sales position to submit to a character-detecting handwriting test devised by Hoosier, but he also had every salesman on the force hypnotized to bust his quota. Or so he thought.

Nathan knew that all the salesmen in the "war room" would *appear* to be "asleep" at this very moment. Some actually were asleep, in the conventional sense. Most were just pretending, waiting for it to be over. But one new fellow had one day literally gone under; he broke all sales records for three consecutive months, until he finally woke up. Outraged at having been *duped* into success, he quit his job and joined the Army.

Nathan went into the sales office to clean out his desk. The sales secretary, a sullen woman in her thirties who never smiled, watched Nathan warily. Office rumor had it that Frick frigged her occasionally in his private office, but Nathan didn't believe it; in his opinion, which he shared freely with his fellow salesmen, even Frick wasn't *that* hard up.

With his arms full of ten years' worth of personal sales detritus, he came back into the demo area and took a seat. The door to the "war room" opened, and a dozen slouching copy machine salesmen filed out like zombies and headed for the streets of Dallas to make cold calls all day long.

"Go get 'em, boys! Sic 'em!" hollered Frick after them. "Think poz-tive, and you will *be* poz-tive!" He turned and looked at Nathan. "You're late," he said. "In fact, you're more than a week late! Where the hell have you been? I've been trying to call you!"

"I've found somebody who wants to pay me $10,000 a month for my piss, so I don't need this fucking, dead-end job anymore."

"You know, Doering, you really *are* crazy! I should have fired your ass five years ago when you threw toner all over that lawyer."

"Frig you Frick! You've made my life miserable for ten years. I'm outta here. Adios, asshole."

Nathan headed for the door, loaded down with "salesman of the month" plaques. On the bright, sunny sidewalk he had a spring in his step. It felt good to quit. At the corner he dumped his plaques into an aluminum can recycling container. Emblazoned on the container was the Lone Star State's official anti-littering slogan: "Don't Mess With Texas!" Below that someone had stuck a popular bumper sticker: "If your heart ain't in Texas, get your ass out!" For the word "heart" was substituted the ubiquitous symbol for the human heart. For the word "ass" was a picture of a wildly bucking jackass.

Nathan drove his trusty old Toyota hatchback toward the East Dallas neighborhood of Casa Linda where he owned a small, frame house within walking distance of White Rock Lake, a sparkling jewel of an oasis in the concrete and asphalt desert that encompassed it. The lake was small by Texas standards, barely a mile across at its widest point and just under three miles long. It lay in the midst of an urban greenbelt of primeval sycamore, pecan, and black willow trees that were nurtured by numerous creeks, all flowing to a confluence in the little body of water.

Nathan had been drawn to the lake immediately upon arriving in Dallas, heartsick and spirit-vexed, twenty years earlier. The White Rock area, with its rolling hills, its shaded creeks, and its wooded parks that surrounded the lake, was the closest thing he could find to the lush, green dells of Virginia that he had reluctantly left behind.

A winding, narrow road encircled the lake, hugging its banks. Between the road and the water, a paved path for joggers and bicyclists followed the shoreline with many twists and curves, through stands of ancient trees and over little wooden bridges spanning the feeder creeks. The trail around the lake was nearly ten miles long.

Overlooking the lake were homes of nearly every description, from rudimentary frame houses that were built in the '30's and '40's as weekend retreats by wealthy city dwellers, to ostentatious mansions such as "Mount Vernon," the palatial homeplace of the now deceased Texas oil billionaire H. L. Hunt. Hunt's widow still lived in the house, which was, more or less, a reproduction of the famous old Virginia home of George Washington. This tacky Texas version of the real Mount Vernon did not make Nathan homesick. It just made him sick.

Nathan's house was not on the lake, but it was nearby. He had managed to buy it in the mid-'70's for practically nothing, just before Dallas real estate prices took off for the moon. At the height of the Texas savings and loan joy ride, it had quadrupled in value. After the jig was up, it had settled somewhere in between. When Nathan bought the house, it had been about to collapse from neglect. It still was. What little discretionary income Nathan had, he spent on books, phonograph records, bicycles, and his sailboat.

Nathan took full advantage of White Rock Lake. He kept fit by riding his bike around the trail nearly every day, and he had spent most of his days off from selling copy machines sailing his fifteen-foot boat up and down and back and forth across the tiny lake. Nathan always sailed alone. He thought of himself as a solo navigator.

Nathan pulled into his driveway in front of the leaning single car garage that was about to fall into his next door neighbor's kitchen. He thought, happily, that with his change in fortune he might at last be able to re-pour the foundation and shore up the garage where it was pulling away from the main part of the house, trying to take the stone chimney with it.

He hid the bottle of formaldehyde under the car seat for safekeeping, grabbed his briefcase, full of sample jars, and went into his house.

The front door opened into a large, pine-paneled living room that occupied fully one-half of the square footage of the house. Nathan lived entirely in this room and the adjoining kitchen and bath. The two bedrooms and den were empty and sealed off. The dilapidated garage was full of the previous owners trash, a broken lawn mower, and rusty garden tools.

Nathan owned little furniture. His bed consisted of a single mattress on an old door that sat up on cinder blocks. Next to the bed was a small table and a reading lamp. There were no chairs, no sofa, no carpet. The floor was littered with books, dirty clothes, record albums, and sailing gear. His bicycle leaned against the picture window that looked out on his overgrown backyard. On one wall was pinned a road map of the state of Virginia. On another wall were three faded snapshots of his baby daughter Rose.

In the kitchen he had a folding card table and a simple wooden chair for dining. He kept his salesman's suits in the bathroom closet. The rest of his clothes and odd possessions were in cardboard boxes lining the living room walls. Nathan was comfortable. It was all he needed.

Nathan changed into jeans, tennis shoes, and a T-shirt. He brushed his teeth, urinated into a fresh sample jar, grabbed his sailbags, and went down to his boat, which he kept in a davit at the sailing club where he was a non-participating member. The club was organized for racers. Nathan was a cruiser. A solitary cruiser.

He lowered his little boat into the water, hanked on the sails, and pushed off. With well-practiced economy of movement, he hoisted the sails, trimmed the sheets, and headed off on a port tack into a warm, southwesterly breeze. He settled back on the cockpit cushion and scanned the sycamore-studded shoreline three quarters of a mile away. After a long, strange, and unsettling week, at last he felt at peace.

Nathan tacked just seconds before reaching the far shore. Coming about smartly, he hauled the main and jib sheets and set his new course close to the wind, paralelling the shoreline so that he could watch the joggers and cyclists on the trail at close range. Many of the faces were familiar: the old, deeply tanned woman with skin like elephant hide, jogging steadily, smiling vacantly through watery-blue eyes (Nathan had never failed to see her on the trail even once in fifteen years of riding his bike); the usual assortment of middle-aged men, huffing and puffing, their jiggling faces contorted in oxygen-starved agony; the deadly-serious, self-important bicycle racers who terrorized preoccupied, strolling lovers with meteor-like close passes and who yielded to no one; the buxom redheaded girl whose bouncing cruise missile breasts occasionally got out of phase with her loping gait and caused her to lose her balance; and the multitude of housewives, their faces caked with make-up, their hair carefully coiffured, their fluorescent spandex workout pants stretched tightly over their cellulite-dimpled buttocks, all doing silly-walks while swinging little red dumbbells in their hands. It was always the same variety show, but Nathan never tired of it.

And then suddenly he saw her . . . the strange little girl . . . or woman . . . on roller skates. She seemed to flow down the path, as if in a dream, with the fluidity and grace of the wind.

He had seen her many times over the past several years. Sometimes when riding his bike he would see her skating toward him down the trail. From a distance she would always appear to be a child of ten or eleven . . . something about the way she moved, and her size . . . but as she would come closer and closer, she would seem to mature almost magically, her small breasts heaving as she breathed, her thewy thighs glistening with sweat in the sunlight . . . and her eyes . . . always staring straight at him, piercing his soul . . . and her smile . . . that enigmatic little half-smile on her unblemished, childlike face that spoke at once of total innocence and yet infinite wisdom.

As Nathan coasted along the shoreline, watching her, she turned her head slowly, looked at him, and smiled. And then she was gone, disappearing like a wood nymph into the ageless trees that shaded the bank of the lake.

EIGHT

Nathan sailed back to the club, secured his boat in its davit, and returned to his house. He packed an assortment of clothes and his toilet articles into a suitcase and filled a small cardboard box with paperback books, including *The Incredible Voyage*, by solo circumnavigator Tristan Jones, and thirteen dog-eared Kurt Vonnegut novels. On the way out, he removed the pictures of Rose from the wall and carefully tucked them between the pages of *God Bless You, Mr. Rosewater*.

When Nathan arrived at the back door of Lucinda's condo in mid-afternoon, Baby Bow Wow was fast asleep in his favorite spot under the dining room table. Nathan entered the kitchen with his hands full and slammed the door shut with his foot. The bang of the door startled Baby Bow Wow, and he instantly sprang into action, running in place at full speed, his sharp little claws laying down ever more fine scratches on Lucinda's polished hardwood floor. Nathan watched him with cool detachment through the archway between the kitchen and dining room, calculating that, with sneakers on his paws, Baby Bow Wow could easily accelerate from a standing start to at least thirty miles per hour in less than six feet.

Baby Bow Wow gained momentum, shot past Nathan with a growl, and darted through the flap in the door . . . *flappity, flap-pity, flap . . . flap*. It was a sound that Nathan would grow to hate.

He put down his suitcase, briefcase, box of books, and bottle of formaldehyde and opened the top freezer door of the refrigerator. He removed the Ziploc bag containing his frozen testicle and placed it on the ceramic tile counter. It made a sound like a marble.

Opening his briefcase, he took out one of the empty urine sample jars and partially filled it with formaldehyde. He opened the Ziploc bag, delicately removed his testicle with his thumb and forefinger, and dropped it into the breathtaking liquid. It sank like a stone.

Nathan screwed on the self-sealing cap tightly and carried the jar into the living room. He looked around for a suitable place to put it. He decided against Lucinda's Early American end tables, and against her antique cobbler's bench coffee table. There really was no choice. It had to be the mantle over the fake Victorian fireplace. With both hands he carefully placed his preserved testicle amid the array of kute 'n kountry knickknacks that Lucinda had thoughtfully arranged there. As Nathan stood back to admire his addition to Lucinda's accessories, the phone rang.

It was Dr. Peter Smith, the urologist and soon-to-be purveyor of aphrodisiacs to lonely men. The meeting with the lawyer was on for four o'clock at Smith's private office at Parkland.

"I'll be there," said Nathan, feeling a twinge of pain in his anus.

"Bring today's urine with you," Dr. Smith reminded him.

"No problem," said Nathan.

Nathan activated his infrared key to open the gate blocking his exit from the compound. He felt annoyed with such paranoid security precautions. As the gate swung slowly open, Pops MacDonald leaned out of the little window of the gatehouse.

"Where you headed, Nathan?" he called.

"To sign the biggest deal of my life!" Nathan called back, smiling at him.

"Atta boy, Nathan!"

Nathan remembered Pops' invitation to visit him for a history lesson on La Coterie. He made a mental note to call on him the next day.

When Nathan arrived at Parkland, Dr. Smith greeted him warmly in his office. The lawyer was late.

"He just called from his car phone," Smith said. "He's on his way."

Nathan turned over his urine and sat down with his back to the door, facing Dr. Smith across his disorderly desk. They chatted about the weather and this and that.

"How are you feeling?" Dr. Smith asked.

"Fine," said Nathan. "Except for this pain in my ass." He had already told Dr. Smith about the vague pelvic throbbing while in the hospital, and about how it had gradually focused into a sharpening pain in his rectum. Dr. Smith had examined his rectum digitally in his hospital bed, much to Nathan's chagrin, and had found nothing wrong. He had told Nathan that the pain was most likely a harmless sympathetic muscular spasm related to the trauma of castration.

Nathan told Dr. Smith about his severe attack at the Pasta Emporium the day before, about how the intense pain had caused him to faint, and about how subsequent twinges seemed to coincide with his state of mind.

"My asshole seems to cramp up whenever something irks me," Nathan complained.

"I don't think there's anything to worry about," said Dr. Smith. "Just try to relax."

Suddenly the door opened, and Smith stood up smiling. "Nathan, I'd like you to meet my attorney, Mr. J. Charleton Skinner, III."

Nathan jumped up from his chair and spun around.

"YOU!" he shouted.

"You?" said Skinner stepping back, dumbfounded.

Nathan spun again and angrily faced the astonished Dr. Smith.

"This is your *lawyer*? Hell! He's nothing but a goddamn sleazeball ambulance chaser!"

"You know each other?" Smith asked.

"Yeah! I know this chickenshit bastard," said Skinner contemptuously. He comes at me in a restaurant yesterday wanting to fight like a *big man* from Ol' Virginny! When I let him know I'm happy to oblige him, he faints like a fairy!"

"You lying motherfucker! I'll . . . . Nathan lunged at Skinner but was drawn up short by another ViseGrip plier lock on his anus. He fell on the floor, writhing in unbearable agony.

"There he goes again!" he heard Skinner say in a faraway, dream-like voice as he lost consciousness once again.

When Nathan came to, the pain was gone. Dr. Smith was stooped over him, holding smelling salts to his nose.

"Now you guys are going to *cool* it!" Smith said authoritatively, looking first at Nathan and then over at Skinner who was standing across the room sulking. "I'm not going to let your personal animosity interfere with this deal! Do you understand me?"

"Why don't you get another lawyer?" Nathan asked. "A *real* lawyer!"

"Shut up, Doering!" snapped Smith. "You don't understand. Charleton is my legal partner in this venture. You've *got* to work with him!"

"Why don't we just get another eunuch?" said Skinner defensively. "A *passive* eunuch!"

"ZIP it, Skinner! Or, I'm warning you, I'll chuck the whole fucking deal and you'll be out on your ass! Now get up, Doering! Let's sign these goddamn documents."

There's nothing quite as persuasive, thought Nathan and Skinner simultaneously, as a furious flamingo with a mission.

Nathan signed away his urine as instructed. Smith forced him to shake Skinner's hand, and he demanded that Skinner apologize to his number one vendor. Then they parted, an uneasy alliance of Dallas entrepreneurs in a bright, new, American venture.

This must be the American Dream that Jimmy McCracken was talking about in his high school valedictory address, thought Nathan as he drove back to his new home at La Coterie.

When he walked in, Lucinda was singing in the kitchen, preparing supper. Baby Bow Wow sat panting at her feet, waiting for a morsel to fall from the chopping block. He growled at Nathan as he entered.

"Hi," said Nathan. "Smells good in here."

"Hi! How was your day?" Lucinda asked happily, looking up from her busy preparations.

"You wouldn't believe it," Nathan said. "I'll tell you about it over dinner." He would tell her about his sail, and possibly about quitting his job. But not about the remarkable Skinner coincidence, of course.

"Baby Bow Wow?" Nathan acknowledged the growling dog squatting on its haunches, its shiny, black balls splayed out on the parquet floor behind him. "Don't get up." He walked in through the dining room and into the living room and put his briefcaseful of new urine sample jars down in a corner.

He looked at the mantle and immediately noticed that his testicle had been replaced by a quilted cloth duck wearing a blue sunbonnet and a lavender shawl. He went over to it and angrily picked it up. It turned out to be a tea cozy . . . his testicle was still there where he had put it, and it now stared out at him from its jar, like the disembodied, dead eye of a Cyclops.

At dinner, Nathan and Lucinda shared the experiences of the day with one another. They talked about many things. But the testicle on the mantle, now snuggled again under its tea cozy, was never mentioned.

NINE

That night Nathan and Lucinda went to bed early, right after dinner. Lucinda excused herself coquettishly, as Nathan undressed, and slipped into the bathroom. She emerged a few minutes later in a new, black satin gown, her thick black hair brushed back from her face, her dark eyes wanton with lust.

Nathan's artistic nature was inspired as never before. He gave Lucinda multiple orgasms with his tongue. Lucinda bit her lips until they bled, trying to subdue the primal screams that welled up from her loins. She succeeded, and Baby Bow Wow slept like a baby under the dining room table. Later, she gratefully, lovingly, tried to reciprocate, gradually bringing Nathan to near-erection. Nathan's heart swelled with joy as his penis at last began to swell with passion. As he approached the orgasm he so madly wanted, so desperately needed, with Lucinda, bless her heart, trying so diligently, so patiently, so persistently . . . . *Flappity, flap-pity, flap . . . flap.*

Nathan's sphincter snapped shut like the bite of a barracuda, and his joy stick went to Jell-O.

Lucinda tried to console him, told him it didn't matter to her, that they would keep trying. She kissed him and held him. She almost told him she loved him.

Nathan finally went to sleep, angry and humiliated, but oddly, not the least bit frustrated.

The next morning after breakfast, Nathan paid a visit to old

Pops MacDonald. He found him in the gatehouse, slumped over in his chair, sound asleep. His hands were in his lap, holding a half-empty pint bottle of gin in a brown paper sack. Nathan tapped him on the shoulder. Pops woke up with a start. He appeared to be completely sober and alert.

"Why, Nathan! How are you, Boy?" he said, genuinely glad to see him. Then he realized that Nathan could see the bottle he was holding. "Have a snort?" He offered the gin to Nathan.

"No, thanks. Little early for me, Pops. Besides, I think I'm a tequila man."

"Ah. Tequila. Can't drink it anymore, Nathan. Knocks me on my butt. Used to, though."

"Are you supposed to be drinking? I thought you were guarding this place."

Pops laughed and set the bottle on his desk, which was nearly covered with surveillance video monitors.

"What's to guard, Nathan? You'd have to be a pole-vaulter to get in this place. Nobody wants in here anyway. Fact is, most of us *in* here want *out*."

"Oh, really? Why's that?"

"Dogs, Nathan. Infernal dogs. They'll drive you crazy with their yapping."

"Yeah," said Nathan. "I've noticed that. They're making quite a racket right now." He and Pops listened attentively. At least a dozen dogs were barking at that very moment. Barking at nothing, thought Nathan peevishly. Just for the hell of it.

"Why is this place so heavily barricaded?" Nathan asked.

"Fear, Nathan. The people here are fearful."

"What are they afraid of?"

"The nightwalkers, mostly, and the homeless folks."

"Nightwalkers?"

"The blacks. After all the tourists go back to their hotels, and the office workers go home for the night, the Negroes come out."

"Come out and do what? Mug people?"

"No, they just walk around. All night long. When the sun comes up, they're gone. Harmless, really. They never hurt anyone. Except the Indian. You gotta watch out for him."

"Indian? What are you talking about?"

"He's an Apache. Half-breed, I think. Calls himself Geronimo. Geronimo Jones. Creeps around the Arts District all night. You gotta watch him. He'll attack you if he gets drunk."

"What the hell are you talking about, Pops? Why do these people walk around all night?"

"Looking for their ancestors. That's what I think."

"Ancestors?"

"Let me tell you about this place, Nathan. When you know the history, I think you'll understand."

"Shoot," Nathan said, eager to learn more. He pulled up a chair.

"La Coterie was the brainchild of Thaddeus Raven," Pops began. "Know who he is?"

"Yes," said Nathan. "Isn't he the housing developer?"

"Right," said Pops. "Built all those subdivisions all over Dallas. Fort Worth, too. Thousands and thousands of houses. All just alike. He's a multi-millionaire. The King of Suburbia. Then he got into commercial real estate. Moved downtown and started buying up property in the seventies just before the boom. He bought this block, where we're sitting right now. He bought it for peanuts. This used to be a rundown industrial area, and there was an old deserted cotton warehouse sitting right here, built around the turn of the century."

"Yes. I remember," said Nathan.

"Well, old Thaddeus, he bided his time. He had a lot to do with getting the new museum built just across the street here. And he made a major donation toward the construction of the symphony center over there." Pops motioned toward the mammoth Myerson music hall on the next block. "Raven had a vision. He was one of the main movers and shakers who created what's now called the Downtown Arts District. The idea was to revitalize downtown Dallas, which was decaying like most other American cities. Everybody moving out to the malls, you know."

"Yes," said Nathan. "It's happening everywhere."

"Right. Well, as I said, the idea was to bring Dallas back, get it back from the blacks, you know, and the homeless. They were moving in like they owned it. And they were trashing it. Especially the blacks."

"The poor, you mean."

"Yeah. The poor blacks. Well, anyway, the plan backfired. Old Thaddeus, he gets the Arts District thing going, and then he tears down the old cotton warehouse to build this place—a 'living center,' he calls it—to bring the whites back in. Unfortunately, he had one little problem."

"What's that?"

"Well, it seems that when they were digging the foundation, they discovered they were sitting smack on top of a graveyard. An old slave graveyard. They found bones and skulls and whole skeletons. Hundreds of 'em. Lots of 'em had their necks broken. Lynchings, you know."

"Jesus! What did they do?" Nathan knew nothing of this incident. But then he never read the newspapers, and he didn't own a television set.

"Well, my belief is that Raven tried to keep it all hush-hush, you know. But the story got out. The newspapers and the TV stations, they had a field day. Then a team of archaeologists came up from Texas A&M and roped the place off. Started pokin' around with their little trowels and brushes, you know, trying to figure out what it was like to be a slave back before the Civil War. The whole black community got their backs up real good about that."

"I can imagine!" said Nathan. "What did they do about it?"

"Well, they got the American Civil Liberties Union on their side. And the Unitarians, too. Finally they forced old Thaddeus to dig 'em up and re-bury 'em over across the Trinity River, over in South Dallas, where all the blacks live. They gave 'em a decent funeral. It was a big to-do. All the city fathers were there."

"That's amazing."

"Yes. But there was something even more amazing. Guess what else those archaeologists found?"

"What?"

"Indian bones. Under*neath* the slaves!"

"Really? You mean an ancient Indian burial ground?"

"No, they weren't all that old. Turns out they were Tonkawas. And it wasn't a burial ground. It was the site of a massacre."

"Jesus! What we did to those innocent, peace-loving people! And we call ourselves civilized!"

"It wasn't us, Nathan. We didn't do it. Those Tonkawas were killed by other Indians. Comanches."

"Comanches? Why?"

"Seems the Tonkawas were nomadic cannibals. The other Indians hated 'em. And when the Tonkawas refused to join forces with them to rub out the white man . . . well, they slaughtered them and left them to rot in the sun . . . right here, right where you're sitting in that chair."

"My God!" said Nathan. He was getting goose bumps.

"That was in 1862," said Pops. He took a swig out of his gin bottle, then offered it again to Nathan. "Sure you won't have a little snort?"

"Don't mind if I do," said Nathan. He took the bottle from Pops, started to take a drink, then stopped. "Wait a minute! Did you say 1862?"

"Yeah, 1862. Right in the middle of the Civil War."

"But you said they were found *under* the slaves!"

"Right."

"But that means the slaves died . . . or were lynched *after* that."

"That figures."

"But, Pops! In 1862, the war was nearly over! The slaves were nearly free! I mean they couldn't *all* have died the day after the Tonkawas were massacred! It would have taken *years* for hundreds of slaves to die and be buried there . . . here, I mean."

"I see your point, Nathan." Pops grew thoughtful. "The only thing I can figure . . . as far as all the lynchings, I mean . . . is that the slaves in Texas weren't told about the Emancipation Proclamation. For that matter, they didn't even know the war was over till years later."

"Are you joking?"

"No, I'm not joking, Boy. They couldn't read. There was no TV. They just didn't know. And nobody was gonna be dumb enough to tell 'em."

"Jesus! That really pisses me off!"

"That's just history, Nathan. Doesn't do any good to rant about history."

"So . . . so these nightwalkers . . . you think they're out trying to communicate with their dead ancestors?"

"Seems like it to me. They just walk around and around the block. They won't talk to you. They won't even look at you. I don't know *what* they're doing. Except the Indian. I think Geronimo's just looking for trouble. You watch out for him, Nathan."

That night after supper, Nathan decided to take a walk.

"Want to join me?" Nathan asked Lucinda.

"No," she said emphatically. "Nathan, I don't think that's a good idea."

"Why not?"

"It's dangerous out there. There are too many creepy people walking around. You could get mugged."

"Pops says they're harmless. He says they're just looking for their long lost relatives."

"You've been talking to Pops?"

"Yeah. He's an interesting old guy. He told me all about the history of this place. About the slave graveyard and the Indian bones."

"He's full of baloney."

"It's not true?"

"Yes, it's true about the graves, but that old sot lets his imagination run away with him. He reads more into things than is really there."

"Well, I'm going. I need some exercise. You're welcome to join me."

"No, thanks. But, Nathan . . . please be careful."

Nathan left La Coterie by the pedestrian gate and started walking down the sidewalk toward the symphony center. It was humid and dark out. He hadn't gone more than twenty feet before he saw his first nightwalker, a tall, thin black man, shabbily dressed and dimly illuminated in the ghostly light of the Victorian-style mercury vapor street lamps. The man passed Nathan silently, like a wraith. He looked straight ahead, as if Nathan didn't exist.

"Good evening," Nathan said. The man didn't answer; he continued straight ahead, then turned, disappearing around the corner. Nathan passed four more shadowy, silent black men before he crossed the street to the symphony center grounds.

The Morton H. Myerson edifice was a huge, box-like building situated in the center of its dedicated block, surrounded by verandas, shrubbery, trees, and lawns intersected by walkways. Near the building on the left, he could see intermittent bursts of blue flame in the darkness, like the flame of a blowtorch, each burst accompanied by riotous laughter. Curious, Nathan approached.

As he came closer, he could see three men, apparently homeless. Nathan made this judgment based on their tattered clothing and their generally unkempt appearance. One of them was bending over, and another was trying to strike a match. After several clumsy tries, the match ignited.

"O.K., let 'er rip!" said the man with the match. Suddenly, to the sound of a flatulent report, a long blue flame tinged with orange and yellow shot out from the bending man's rear end; whereupon, all three men cheered loudly and laughed, coughing and wheezing, till they cried. One of them even fell down from laughing so hard.

My God, they're lighting their farts! Nathan realized with alarm. He thought about the teen-aged boy with his Zippo lighter, and he ran up to the men.

"Stop! Stop!" Nathan shouted. "That's extremely dangerous!"

The men stopped laughing and drew back, frightened by Nathan's sudden intrusion.

"We're not doing anything," one of the men said defensively. "We're not hurting anybody!"

"You're going to hurt *yourself* doing that!" Nathan said. "I know somebody who burned their balls up doing that!"

"Bullshit!" said the man who had struck the match. "We do this all the time!"

"Why?" Nathan asked, incredulous.

"For fun! What *else* is there to do in this fucking town?"

"Please believe me!" Nathan pleaded. "You can really hurt yourself!"

"Hey, Buddy." One of the men came up to Nathan. His breath reeked of cheap wine. "Can you spare a dollar or two? We haven't eaten all day."

"I'm . . . I'm sorry . . . I don't have any money with me," Nathan stammered, digging in his pockets. It was true. He had left his wallet back at the condo.

"Well, how about a cigarette then?"

"I'm sorry . . . I don't smoke."

"Then get the hell outta here and leave us alone!" one of the men said. "We're not bothering you or anybody else."

The third man, who had unzipped his filthy pants, was urinating on an exotic Oriental bush in a planter. "Yeah!" he said. "Buzz off, Buster!"

Nathan left quickly. He walked as fast as he could back to La Coterie, went into the condo, found his wallet on the cobbler's bench coffee table, and went out again without speaking to Lucinda. He returned to the symphony center and found the three homeless men still there. To their astonishment, he gave each of them a one hundred dollar bill.

"I'm sorry, I . . . I didn't mean to bother you," Nathan said. He turned before they could reply and walked back toward La Coterie, where he was about to be ambushed.

TEN

"**H**I-YAAAAAAH!!!"

Nathan heard the sudden, hair-raising cry come from above and behind him. Before he could take evasive action, a massive weight fell on his shoulders, and he was slammed down hard on the sidewalk. A strong hand pulled his head back violently by the hair, and a pair of fat legs sheathed in fringed Naugahyde held his torso in a crushing scissors lock. Nathan struggled desperately to free himself from his attacker's iron grip. Twisting and writhing, he was able at last to turn enough to see a large, round face with smoldering eyes and a sinister, smiling mouth. A bolt of lightning, drawn jaggedly with bright yellow Day-Glow magic marker, shot down from one eye, across a large aquiline nose, to a chubby, hairless chin.

It was Geronimo Jones.

"Got you! Paleface motherfucker!" cried Geronimo. He suddenly released Nathan and sprang to his feet. "Now it your turn, Corporal!" His knife flashed in the eerie light from the street lamp as it sliced through the crotch in Nathan's trousers, barely missing his penis.

"Take *that*, Corporal Williams!"

"Wait! Please!" Nathan whined, nearly paralyzed with terror. "You've got me confused with someone else! I'm not a corporal! I've never been in the Army! I'm 4-F!" This was true. Nathan's brief stay in the Medical College of Virginia psycho ward had disqualified him for armed service.

Geronimo ignored his plea and lunged at his crotch, ripping

open his trousers where he had cut the fabric. He grabbed the elastic waistband of Nathan's underpants and jerked, tearing them off his body.

"Help!" Nathan screamed. "Please! Somebody! Help me!"

Geronimo slugged him with his fist, dazing him. He roughly grabbed Nathan's scrotum with his left hand, holding the knife in his right, poised to strike again. But sensing something was wrong, he released the empty scrotum. Confused, he grabbed it again, massaging the mucilaginous sack, investigating its contents with his pudgy Apache fingers. Suddenly the truth dawned on Geronimo: This man was already castrated!

"You not be Corporal Williams?"

"No!" Nathan whimpered, still dizzy from the blow to his head.

"But you yellowhair. Like Custer. Like Corporal Williams."

"No . . . please . . . I . . . ."

"Eyes blue. Like sky."

"Please! Let me go!"

Geronimo released Nathan's scrotum. "You not be in Vietnam?"

"No! I've never been out of the United States! Please! Put the knife down!"

Geronimo dropped the knife on the sidewalk. He looked befuddled, disappointed.

"My name is Nathan Doering. I'm a . . . I was a copy machine salesman. I sold Fuller Brushes door-to-door during the Vietnam War. You've got me mixed up with someone else."

Geronimo dropped to his knees and bowed his big head. "Forgive me, Kemosabi." He began to cry. "You brother," he sobbed. "You eunuch like Geronimo."

There was sudden movement behind Geronimo. A sickening thud. And the half-breed Apache slumped to the pavement, unconscious and bleeding.

It was Pops MacDonald with his riot baton.

Pops wanted to call the police. Nathan protested, insisted that they take Geronimo to the gatehouse, revive him, tend his split scalp. "He called me 'Kemosabi,'" Nathan said.

"I warned you to watch out for this crazy son of a bitch," Pops complained as they laboriously dragged Geronimo's two hundred and fifty pound bulk down the sidewalk toward the gate. Inside, they laid the huge Indian out on the floor of the gatehouse. Pops got a wet rag, and they squeezed water on his face, causing the lightning flash to run down into his ears in yellow rivulets. Geronimo finally came around. Nathan lifted his head, and Pops poured gin in his mouth.

"Um! Firewater good!" said Geronimo.

"Are you O.K.?" Nathan asked.

"Head hurt! Geronimo hit with tomahawk?"

"Quit talking like Tonto, you idiot!" said Pops. He'd had encounters with Geronimo Jones in the past, and he knew it was an act. The Indian had been arrested at least twice outside La Coterie's gates and jailed for assault and battery. Pops knew he talked like a retardate so the cops would go easy on him.

Nathan and Pops disinfected Geronimo's bleeding scalp with gin. A true Apache, he withstood the stinging stoically.

"Who is Corporal Williams?" Nathan asked.

Geronimo's eyes clouded over. "Paleface motherfucker!" He spat on the floor.

"Geronimo, please. Tell me. What did he do to you?" Nathan was bursting with curiosity, compassion, empathy. "Did he castrate you?"

"What?!" exclaimed Pops.

"Is that what he did, Geronimo?" Nathan put his hand compassionately on the fat Indian's thigh.

"Yes. In effect . . . that's what he did. And if I ever find him, I will have my revenge! I will cut his balls off in the old Apache way! The ancient Indian way!"

"The Apaches never mutilated anybody till the Spaniards showed 'em how," said Pops. "There ain't no such thing as 'the old Apache way.' Read your history books, Geronimo!"

"Knock it off, Pops! Can't you see this man has been brutalized?" Nathan pulled up a chair and sat down facing Geronimo.

"Tell me what happened. Was it in Vietnam?"

"Yes." Geronimo closed his eyes, thinking back to his painful past. "Williams was my platoon leader. He was a racist. He called me Tonto. Tonto, do this. Tonto, do that!"

"'Tonto' is the Spanish word for stupid," said Pops.

"Pops! Let it *be!*" Nathan said angrily. "Go on, Geronimo."

"He actually thought that because I'm part Indian I had natural scouting ability," Geronimo continued. "He thought I was genetically better at sneaking. So . . . so he always sent me in first . . . always forced me to be the first one down a jungle trail . . . like I could *smell* the mines with my big Indian nose or something. I told him I was just like everybody else. I told him I was scared. He just laughed. *Laughed* at me . . . and made me go anyway."

Geronimo fell silent. Tears rolled down his bronze, Day-Glow-streaked face.

"What happened, Geronimo?"

"What do you think? My luck ran out. I finally stepped on a mine and blew my balls off. Half my dick went with 'em."

"Christ!" said Nathan.

Pops took a big swill of gin, emptying the bottle. He opened a drawer in his desk and took out a sealed fifth of Beefeaters. He opened it and held it out.

"Have a snort, boys."

Nathan, Pops, and Geronimo Jones sat up in the gatehouse of La Coterie until three a.m. and got blind, stinking drunk. They talked and cried and told jokes. At one point, Pops happened to look down at Nathan's crotch and saw his scarred, deflated scrotum through the opening in his cut and ripped trousers. Nathan let him have a good look, told all about his encounter with Baby Bow Wow, and then he and Geronimo drunkenly compared what was left of their genitals to the fascination and merriment of all.

Pops, not to be outdone, even dropped *his* pants to show his "boys" his birthmark: One side of his penis and half his pubic hair was dead white due to a pigmentation deficiency.

They all laughed and had another pull on the gin bottle.

After Pops passed out on the floor, Geronimo told Nathan the sad story of his return to Dallas from Vietnam. He had been in good shape before he stepped on that land mine, lean and athletic. But within six months in convalescence he had ballooned into obesity. He had not been able to get a job. If he wasn't discriminated against for being an Indian, he was discriminated against for being fat. Finally, in desperation he had taken a job at minimum wage as a janitor at The Cockpit, a homosexual bar in the infamous Cedar Springs area of Dallas.

He worked hard at his job and gradually slimmed down. Eventually he was promoted to the position of stage manager at The Lavender Ballroom, an upstairs adjunct to the bar where transvestites danced on stage for tips. When he got back down to his normal weight, he was offered the opportunity to perform on stage as "Pocahontas" in a baby blue buckskin bikini. He took the job and made nearly three times his previous salary in tips. Geronimo, it turned out, was a good dancer. With his long, black, natural braids and his hairless, pear-shaped body, he was a hit at The Cockpit.

But the years took their toll. He began drinking heavily and got fat again. The audiences started laughing at him rather than applauding and tipping him. At last he was put back on his old job as stage manager, where he still worked on weekends. Monday through Thursday, he told Nathan, he slept all day and prowled the streets of the Arts District at night, looking for Corporal Williams and hanging out with the homeless winos.

But to Nathan, the real clincher to Geronimo's miserable existence was the fact that what little money he earned at The Cockpit he gave to Brother Larry Proffitt in advance payment for the miracle of genital reincarnation, a miracle, of course, which never came.

"Does Proffitt know what you're giving him your money for?" Nathan asked. He was outraged at this revelation.

"Yes. Brother Larry knows everything. I wrote him a long letter telling him what happened to me in Vietnam and what my problems are. And I've called him many times and talked with his telephone prayer ministers. They are very kind and understanding. Brother Larry wrote back to me and told me that God is angry with me and is punishing me for my sins. He said the only way I can be forgiven is to plant my seeds of faith and to pay my vows. So I plant, and I pay. But things seem to be getting worse and worse for me. I guess God is still very angry with me."

"Geronimo, for God's sake! Can't you see you're being ripped off by a charlatan? This bastard would sell his own mother to the devil for five bucks!" Nathan tried to explain how the Faith 'N Fortune racket worked, how it preyed upon downtrodden, desperately unhappy people by first telling them their misfortune in life was a result of their own despicable morality and then offering to sell them redemption for what little money they had.

"I know it's a long shot," Geronimo said. "But it's the only chance I've got."

Nathan made Geronimo promise he would go with him the next day to see Dr. Peter Smith.

"I think he can help you more than Larry Proffitt can," Nathan said. "At least he can give you testosterone shots. Or, just maybe, he can give you a better job."

ELEVEN

When Nathan got back to the condo at about four a.m., Lucinda was still up, sitting on the sofa in her robe. She glared at Nathan as he came in the door.

"Where the hell have you been? I've been worried sick about you. I was getting ready to call the police. What in God's name happened to your pants?! What have you been up to?!"

Nathan, still shaky from the gin, told Lucinda all about Geronimo Jones, how the big Indian had jumped him and tried to castrate him, how he had burst into tears when he realized Nathan was already a eunuch like him, how Pops had split his head open with his riot baton, and all about their long conversation.

"I'm going to try to get him help," Nathan said.

Then he told her about the nightwalkers he'd seen, and about the homeless men lighting their farts at the symphony hall. And how he'd come back to get money for them when he'd breezed in and out without speaking.

"This is really just a bit much, Nathan," Lucinda said tiredly. "I'm going to bed."

She did, and Nathan spent what was left of the night curled up on the sofa.

The next morning, after Lucinda left for the gallery, Nathan called Dr. Smith and made an appointment for Geronimo Jones.

"I've met a fellow who I think you'd like to meet," said Nathan into the phone. "He's testosterone-free, like me, and he needs money worse than I do. Can you use another eunuch?"

"I need all the pure urine I can get," said Dr. Smith. "How's eleven o'clock?"

"We'll be there," Nathan said.

Nathan drove to the address Geronimo had written on a scrap of paper and given to him the night before. He lived in a rundown, seedy part of town in a one-room apartment over a garage that was in worse shape than the one pulling away from Nathan's house.

There was no answer when Nathan knocked, so he opened the door and went in. Geronimo was asleep on the floor, still dressed in his Naugahyde, fringed Indian pants. Nathan woke him, cleaned him up, and drove him to Parkland in his Toyota hatchback.

Geronimo and Dr. Smith hit it off immediately. Smith took a urine specimen, left his office for fifteen minutes to personally analyze it, returned smiling, and explained the deal. Geronimo accepted his unexpected miracle with eudaemonia, kissed Dr. Smith's hand, and took a check for $5,000 in advance payment for one month's urine.

Nathan and Geronimo left with a fresh supply of urine jars and went shopping. They bought new clothes for Geronimo, went to the barber, opened a checking account in the name of Jones at Nathan's bank, and dined at the Pasta Emporium to celebrate their good fortune.

Geronimo told Nathan he didn't want to quit his job at The Cockpit. He said the only friends he had were the transvestites who danced there. In fact, he said, he wanted Nathan to meet his best friend, Michael-Michelle.

"She's a beautiful dancer, Nathan," said Geronimo. His voice was full of admiration. "She dances for art. She's the only dancer at The Lavender Ballroom who refuses tips."

"How does she make a living?" Nathan asked.

"Oh, she's . . . he's a very successful fashion photographer here in Dallas. Michael Davidson. He has a huge studio in the Arts District. He's very well-off. In fact, I don't know how I would have made it all these years without his help. I really love that man. Platonically, I mean. I'm not gay. Nathan, if that's what you thought."

"It never crossed my mind, Geronimo."

Geronimo invited Nathan to come to The Lavender Ballroom at 10 p.m. that night to catch Michael-Michelle's act.

Nathan said he would come.

That evening over dinner, Lucinda excitedly told Nathan about plans for Vincent D'Amato's one-man show at her gallery, the art debut of the decade, an art happening that would knock the socks off the Dallas avant-garde culture clique.

"Vincent has come up with an absolutely brilliant idea, Nathan," Lucinda said. "But, of course, that is *so* characteristic of him. He is such an *incredible* genius!"

"Let me guess," said Nathan. "He's going to commit performance-art suicide in front of all your phony art patron socialites."

"You know, Nathan, sometimes I think you're jealous. You never have anything nice to say about art. You make jokes about my gallery . . . about the artists I represent. And you, of all people! Nathan Doering, the *quintessential* artist!" Lucinda feigned a little pout with her full, sensuous lips.

God, she's sexy, thought Nathan. "I apologize," he said. "What's his idea?"

"You're not going to believe this, Nathan!" Lucinda was more ebullient than he had ever seen her. "I'm turning over my entire gallery to him. I'm stripping it bare, putting everything in the basement. Including the furniture, the carpets, everything! He's going to transform the gallery *itself* into a work of art! Walls, ceiling, floor . . . the entire building! All new work! He says he can do it in a week! Can you believe it? He's promised that he will create his ultimate statement on the world . . . on reality itself . . . right in my gallery! He's like a wild animal! I've never seen such artistic passion! I'm going to turn him loose in the morning!"

"Lucinda," Nathan said with concern, "are you sure this is a smart thing to do? With all due respect to his 'genius,' this guy sounds like he's crazy. He could destroy your gallery!"

"He's not violent, Nathan. He doesn't destroy things. He creates! He is so *incredibly* spontaneous! I *know* what I'm doing, Nathan. I'm *never* wrong when it comes to artistic genius! I simply cannot *wait* to watch him in action!"

After dinner, Lucinda wanted to make love. In the storm-tossed waterbed she performed and responded with unbridled abandon to the brilliant ministrations of *Nathan's* genius, barely managing to suppress her screams. It occurred to Nathan that her wires of sexual arousal and artistic appreciation, now stimulated by the prospect of D'Amato's upcoming show, were somehow crossed . . . or at least interconnected.

(Nancy, his ex-wife, had displayed a similar phenomenon of eroto-intellectual confusion in the late '60's. An ardent pacifist and strident critic of the war in Vietnam, she had demonstrated frequently and passionately in the streets of Richmond while he stayed at home babysitting their daughter Rose. On her returns from the nonviolent confrontations with hawkish authority, sweaty and feverish with moral outrage, she had invariably ravished him like a tigress in heat.)

At Lucinda's peak of erotic frenzy, with Nathan closer than ever to full erection, she tried to effect penetration. But, in the short journey from mouth to vulva, Nathan's penis retreated like a frightened bunny into the underbrush of his golden pubic hair.

While Lucinda again assured him that it mattered not at all to her, Nathan nevertheless sensed for the first time her disappointment.

Nathan dressed and left Lucinda, flushed and tingling but (he feared) unfulfilled, on the rumpled sheets of the undulating waterbed. He was off to watch Michael-Michelle dance on The Lavender Ballroom stage at The Cockpit, Dallas' finest homosexual nightspot.

Downstairs, Baby Bow Wow growled at him from his spot under the dining room table as he passed through toward the kitchen door.

"Come on, you little prick!" Nathan said to the dog. "Hunch *my* leg! I'll kick your nasty little nuts to pulp!"

On his way out of La Coterie, Nathan stopped short of the gate and parked. He went into the gatehouse to see Pops MacDonald. He carried four Kurt Vonnegut novels with him, which he planned to lend the old man to help him pass the time. He also was curious to see if Pops had survived the drunken party of the previous night; he had still been passed out on the floor when Nathan and Geronimo had finally left.

Pops was seated in his chair with his head resting on a surveillance video monitor on his desk. He was not asleep, but he was badly hung over.

"Pops!" Nathan greeted him. "I've brought you some books to read."

"Uhhh . . . Nathan, boy." Pops raised his head, holding his hands to his temples, and looked up at Nathan.

"How are you, Pops? Looks like you need a little hair of the dog that bit you!"

"On, no, Nathan. I'll never drink again. Never. I've got the worst headache I've ever had in my life. I just want to die."

"Here," Nathan said, handing him the books. "These novels will make you want to go on living. I hope you'll read them."

Pops took the books and looked at their covers. "Vonnegut. Science fiction, huh? I don't go in much for science fiction, Nathan."

"It's not science fiction, Pops. It's truth. It's raw humanity. Vonnegut's the most serious, truthful novelist writing today. Read 'em, Pops. These books will change your life."

"I don't want my life changed, Boy. I just want it to end. Ahhh . . . my head is throbbing."

"Well then read 'em for fun. They'll make you laugh. They're all short and easy."

"I can't read anything now. I can hardly see."

"Well, I gotta go. Get a good night's sleep. You'll be a new man tomorrow."

"Where you off to, Nathan?"

"Goin' to watch some fancy dancin', Pops."

"Atta boy, Nathan!"

TWELVE

Nathan drove his Toyota hatchback up and down Cedar Springs Avenue, along the notorious strip of homosexual bars, clothing boutiques, antique shops, book stores, and cafés. Finally he spotted The Cockpit, a modest two-story building flanked on one side by The Book Nook, a small store that advertised "Designer Incense and Unguents" and "Homophilic Literature and Novelties," and on the other side by a lingerie shop called The Pink Orchid that offered not only corsets, negligees, and naughty lace panties, but leather goods for bondage and masquerade as well.

Nathan parked and walked, with some trepidation, toward The Cockpit . . . and his ultimate destination . . . The Lavender Ballroom upstairs. The mostly male crowd that thronged the sidewalks and spilled out onto the street amongst the traffic was in a party mood. Nathan was jostled by tough-looking men dressed as cowboys and motorcycle punks. He was looked over licentiously by small, tightly clustered groups of young men in full feminine attire, mincing and pantomiming exaggerated female gestures. But, by far, the majority of the crowd were rather ordinary-looking men and boys with their pants hitched up to create codpieces for their genitals. Most of them appeared to possess enormous organs. One in particular, Nathan thought, had surely stuffed his trousers with something . . . a sock, a towel, a cucumber, a salami . . . something else. The murmur of the crowd was punctuated now and then by little shrieks and squeals of great good humor.

Nathan maneuvered his way through the milling, warm testosterone factory and stopped before the meretriciously decorated display window of The Pink Orchid. The window was filled with androgynous mannequins. Some wore garishly colored, diaphanous silk and nylon nothings; positioned in surrealistic but suggestive postures, they seemed suspended in a kind of elastic tension by a maze of garters, cinches, and straps. Other mannequins stood, stiff-legged, among them, one masked with a tight-fitting, black leather hood; they wore an assortment of spike-studded collars, belts, cuffs, gloves, vests, and chaps. Placed here and there on their fiberglass bodies were various mysterious leather straps and metal rings, the function of which Nathan was not sure he fully understood.

What he did understand, however, was the function of a device worn by one of the lingerie mannequins: a black leather ball stuffed into its open mouth, held in place by a strap that buckled behind its head. Nathan thought he would like to buy one of those for Baby Bow Wow.

Nathan walked on past the entrance to The Cockpit and looked in the window of the "homophilic" Book Nook next door. Prominently displayed was the newest self-help "bestseller," a slim volume entitled *30 Days To Comely Buns*. On its cover was a rear view illustration of a young man in skintight jeans, slightly steatopygous, but otherwise muscular and handsome, looking back over his shoulder, a come-hither smile on his youthful, epicene face.

"God loves you, Brother!"

Nathan was startled by the distinctly female voice behind him. He turned to face a demented-looking woman of about twenty-five. She was cock-eyed, and she held a tattered Bible tightly to her breast in the studied, ecclesiastical fashion.

"Stop the perversion now!" she implored Nathan. "Fornography killeth! It destroyeth the soul of man! So saith the Lord!"

Nathan noticed that she wore a large laminated button on her blouse. The button bore the smiling visage of Brother Larry Proffitt, and the words: "Faith 'N Fortune Urban Outreach Mission."

"You pornicateth, you burneth in hell!" said the woman, her wandering eye blazing with religious condemnation.

"My problem," Nathan replied, "is that I couldn't pornicate even if I wanted to."

"Huh?"

"I'm a eunuch."

"Huh?"

"I've been castrated. You know. Snip-snip." Nathan made a scissors-like motion with his fingers at his crotch.

"You don't have no pornicator?"

"Well, yes. But it no longer pornicateth. A satanic little dog biteth my balls . . . biteth my only testicle off."

"Ouch!"

"To say the least. But, tell me, Sister, why do you think God would let such a thing happen to me? Is God angry with me?"

"You have sinned, Brother."

"But I'll bet you know a way that I can be forgiven, right?"

"Oh, yes, Brother! Praise the Lord!" The woman dropped to her knees on the sidewalk and began to pray. "Oh, Lord, in the name of sweet GEE-zus, save this sinner! Pray with me, Brother!" She grabbed Nathan by his belt and pulled him down on his knees. She was amazingly strong. "Quo-dah-bah-sah-tah! Kashanda! Bohtanda! Doh-boh-duh-soy-yuh! PRAY with me, Brother!"

"Ree-doo-koo!" said Nathan.

"Oh, YES, Lord! He speaketh your anointed word! Restoreth the angels to this repentant pornicator!"

"Can God really give me back my angels?" Nathan asked.

"God worketh in mysterious ways!"

"You can say *that* again!"

"God worketh in mysterious . . . .:

"How can I get my balls back, Sister?"

"Plant a seed of faith, Brother." She opened her Bible and removed a Faith 'N Fortune brochure covered with pictures of Brother Proffitt in action . . . praying, prophesying, healing, exhorting, banishing the devil. The brochure asked the searing questions, "Who is this man?" and "What is his mission?" She thrust it into Nathan's hands.

"Read this, Brother," she said, "and follow the instructions. God will heal you!"

Nathan, still on his knees, skimmed the brochure while the woman continued to pray for the expulsion of his demons of iniquity. Following an explanation of the "seed of faith" rationale and a short paragraph on the divine necessity of paying one's vows in a timely fashion, the brochure offered a checklist of miraculously curable ailments . . . everything from venereal diseases to heart trouble to AIDS.

"Can Larry Proffitt cure AIDS, too?" asked Nathan, nearly choking with rage.

"Oh, yes! Praise the Lord! Through God's special anointing, Brother Larry can cure anything! Are you cursed with AIDS, too, Brother?"

Nathan stood up and threw the brochure in her face.

"You miserable, stupid bitch! Don't you know that you're working for a crook who will stoop to anything to make a fast buck?"

"BLASPHEMY!!" yelled the woman, jumping to her feet.

"Larry Proffitt is a heartless, pandering motherfucker! He's killing people with his greed! He's killing them with fear! He's killing them with God!"

"Oh, sweet GEE-zus!" The woman thrust her Bible heavenward. "Smite this evil pornicator! Burn him in hell! BURN HIM!!"

A silent crowd of homosexuals was now forming, pressing in around them, witnessing with mouths agape an epic battle between good and evil.

"It's Larry Proffitt who should burn in hell!" cried Nathan. "The devil looks like Mother Teresa next to that bastard!"

"BLASPHEMY!! BLASPHEMY!!"

Suddenly the crowd parted, and a man in a business suit stepped in and separated Nathan and the hysterical Faith 'N Fortune missionary.

"Get out of here, you crazy goddamned kook!" the man said to the dim-witted proselytizer. "I told you if I caught you out here again I'd call the cops! Now SCRAM!"

The man turned and faced Nathan. It was J. Charleton Skinner, III.

"Skinner!" Nathan exclaimed.

"Doering?"

"What are *you* doing here?" Nathan asked, smirking.

"I might ask you the same thing, Smartass!"

"Why, Jay! I didn't know you were gay!"

Skinner looked around at the attentive ring of homosexuals watching them. "Move on," he told them. "It's all over. Move along. You're blocking the entrance." He turned back to Nathan. "I'm not gay, Smartass. I manage this business."

"The Book Nook?"

"No. The Cockpit. What are you doing here?"

"Well, I've got to hand it to you, Skinner. For a sleazeball lawyer, you're incredibly versatile . . . ambulance chaser, counsel for a sick-o aphrodisiac manufacturer, manager of a gay bar . . . . Is there no limit to your nefarious activities?"

"A rolling stone gathers no moss," Skinner said.

"Yeah. Just slime."

"Now look, Smartass! I'm willing to be civil to you, even though I hate your fucking guts, but you've got to make an effort, too. I know how Smith thinks. He really *will* dump us if we don't get along. We're talking big money here, Doering."

"O.K. Forget it."

"What *are* you doing here? Why were you tormenting that religious idiot?"

"*She* accosted *me*! I've got a serious problem with that Proffitt bastard. Please tell me you don't work for him, *too*!"

"Never met the guy. But I must admit he's got a sweet little deal going for himself. Wouldn't mind a piece of his action."

"Someone really ought to assassinate that motherfucker!"

"You know, Doering, I think you're basically a dangerous person. You need to control that temper of yours. You can get into a lot of trouble the way you mouth off."

"Dangerous? I'll tell you who's dangerous! Proffitt is bilking poor people out of their grocery money! But worse than that, he's selling them false hope! He's killing people by selling them faith and hope in a god he can't possibly believe in himself."

"You've really got a burr up your ass, don't you, Doering?"

Nathan involuntarily contracted his sphincter. He suddenly realized that his anus had been killing him for the last ten minutes.

"Let me ask you again," Skinner said. "What are you doing down here?"

"I came to see the show. The dancers. Geronimo Jones invited me."

"You know Geronimo?"

"I gather you haven't talked to Smith today," Nathan said.

"No. Why?"

"I took Geronimo to his office this morning. Smith signed him up. He's buying his piss, too."

"Geronimo? He's a . . . a eunuch?"

"You didn't know?"

"No. I didn't. But I'm not surprised, now that I think about it. I always thought there was something strange about him . . . besides being queer, I mean."

"Geronimo is *not* a homosexual."

"Hey! We're talking Pocahontas here! He used to dance upstairs in a G-string!"

"He did it for money, Skinner! The poor guy's been shit on all his life. He got his balls and his dick blown off in Vietnam because of some racist platoon leader! He couldn't get a decent job because he was an Indian! Because he was fat! He's been brutalized all his life! And now he's being raped by Larry Proffitt! Did you know he's been paying Proffitt every last cent he earns here to have God miraculously give him back his privates?"

"No. I didn't know that." Skinner frowned with what seemed to Nathan a genuine concern for Geronimo. "Maybe somebody *ought* to assassinate that little pope! I like Geronimo. He's a good guy. A good employee."

"Yeah. I like him, too," said Nathan.

"Come on," said Skinner. "I'll take you upstairs."

101

THIRTEEN

As Skinner led Nathan through the darkened lounge of The Cockpit, between tables of men seated and drinking together, between standing couples hugging and dancing in the aisles, someone pinched Nathan on his left buttock. He whirled around, furious, ready to fight, but it was impossible to tell who had done it. After glaring at several men who seemed likely suspects, Nathan finally turned and angrily followed Skinner up the carpeted stairs to The Lavender Ballroom.

The ballroom was huge, occupying the entire second floor of the building. Softly lit by crystal chandeliers, it was truly lavender. Lavender walls and ceiling, lavender carpet surrounding the expansive dance floor in the center of the room, lavender upholstered chairs, lavender tablecloths, and a lavender lamé stage curtain.

The dance floor was packed. Unlike the slow-moving, swaying dancers in the dark downstairs, these men and their drag queen partners were *serious* dancers. The atmosphere was frenetic and joyous. The music was upbeat, with a strongly pulsed rhythm, and the dancers swooped and swirled with energy and precision. Oddly, nearly all of the drag queens were Cher look-alikes.

The stage was at the far end of the ballroom. About fifty small tables with four chairs each, nearly all occupied, were clustered in front of the stage apron. On stage, three black transvestites, all gussied up in designer party dresses, wigs, make-up, and gaudy jewelry, were cavorting like spastic automatons.

"What kind of dancing is that?" Nathan asked Skinner.

"They call it vogue-ing," Skinner said. "Doesn't do much for me."

"I don't like it either."

"Wait till you see Michael-Michelle. He's fantastic!"

"That's who I came to see," Nathan said.

Skinner found Nathan a table to himself and went back down to The Cockpit to take care of business. Nathan ordered a drink from a cute little transvestite waiter in a frilly white apron, black pantyhose, and a lavender satin bow tie. He settled back in his lavender, velvet-upholstered French provincial chair and watched the show.

After the black voguers finished their routine, a series of still more Cher look-alikes, dressed in revealing lingerie, took turns strutting lewdly about the stage, caressing intimate parts of their own bodies, and leering at the appreciative audience. To Nathan, it was fun to watch, but it was not dancing.

Suddenly the lights dimmed, the lavender lamé curtain descended, and the music stopped. The dancers on the ballroom dance floor became still, and a hush fell over the audience. Geronimo Jones, dressed in the new suit that Nathan had helped him select that afternoon, walked out on the stage.

"Ladies and gentlemen," he said in a clear voice, "it is my privilege to present to you The Queen of The Lavender Ballroom, Michael-Michelle! Let's give her a big hand!"

The audience, including Nathan, applauded enthusiastically. Geronimo left the stage, and the curtain rose again to the opening strains of Rimsky-Korsakov's "Scheherazade."

Like an apparition of unearthly grace and loveliness, Michael-Michelle emerged from the wings and fairly floated across the stage, her long flaxen hair shimmering in the spotlight, her silken, pale blue gown of veils clinging to her lithe body and drifting after her like gossamer. Her classic alabaster face, radiant and sensual; her eyes . . . now demure . . . now flashing . . . now tragic; her delicate hands, like white doves in flight; her bare, slender, pale feet gliding, carrying her supple body lightly across the floor—all combined in exquisite harmony and symmetry, expressing the tender, passionate, wistful, and melancholy emotions of that celestial music.

Nathan was moved nearly to tears.

At intermission, Geronimo escorted Michael-Michelle to Nathan's table.

"Michael-Michelle, this is my new friend, Nathan Doering. He saved my life today." Geronimo's pudgy chin was dimpled and quivering with emotion.

"I am so pleased to meet you, Nathan." Michael-Michelle offered her hand.

"The pleasure is mine," said Nathan. He took her hand and gallantly kissed it. Her skin was soft as a child's and smelled faintly of gardenias.

Michael-Michelle blushed and sat down in the chair nearest Nathan. She wore no make-up other than light eye shadow. Her complexion was clear and fresh, her forehead and upper lip lightly beaded with perspiration from the exertion of her dance.

"That's the first time anyone ever kissed my hand," she said. "It was very sweet of you."

"You are the most beautiful dancer I have ever seen in my life," said Nathan. "Thank you for sharing your art."

Well, I've got to get backstage," Geronimo interrupted. He was beaming with happiness. "You two have a good time getting to know each other."

Nathan and Michael-Michelle talked for nearly two hours. Nathan told her right off the bat that he was castrated, and he told her how it happened. She listened in astonishment. She was sympathetic.

Michael-Michelle told Nathan that dancing was the most important thing in her life, that she practiced five hours each day in her photography studio, that she had spent years perfecting her art, studying the choreography of her idol, Martha Graham. She told him that she dreamed of being a woman, that she felt closest to realizing her dream when she was dancing in her silken veils.

Nathan recited lines from one of his favorite poems by Robert Herrick:

> *Whenas in silks my Julia goes,*
> *Then, then (methinks) how sweetly flows*
> *That liquefaction of her clothes.*

"Yes. That's it exactly," said Michael-Michelle. "The liquefaction . . . the flow . . . the touch of silken fabrics on my skin. It makes me feel so feminine . . . so womanly."

"Have you considered . . . an operation?" Nathan asked tentatively. He was half-afraid he might be committing a faux pas.

"You mean a sex change. Yes. I'm considering it now. But I'm terribly frightened."

"Well . . . what's involved . . . I mean what exactly is involved in doing that?"

"The first step is quite pleasurable. I'm going through that now."

"Through what?"

"Well, the first year . . . before the actual operation . . . you take estrogen injections. I've been on estrogen for nine months now. And you wear women's clothing at all times . . . the more feminine the better. This is the pre-feminizing stage . . . to help prepare you for the operation . . . psychologically as well as physically."

"What effect has it had on you?"

"Psychologically, not much. I've always *felt* like a woman. Physically, there have been some rather striking changes. My hips have enlarged. I'm getting a figure. And I'm developing breasts. I can't tell you what a joy that is, Nathan."

Nathan could not overcome his impulse to look at Michael-Michelle's breasts. Through the thin, clinging blue veil in which she was sheathed, he could clearly discern the soft protrusions of her budding nipples.

"I've never had much body hair," said Michael-Michelle. "I'm so fair, you see. But now I have practically none. I haven't needed to shave in six months. Except for my legs and armpits, of course," she blurted. Both Michael-Michelle and Nathan blushed at that, and then they laughed together. "Here, feel my arm," she said. Nathan stroked her forearm. It was smooth . . . with a light, golden down . . . like a pre-pubescent child's.

"That's really remarkable," said Nathan. He looked admiringly at her as she tossed her long, fine, blond hair back over her delicate shoulders. "You are very beautiful."

"Thank you, Nathan. That means a lot to me for you to say that."

"What about the operation? What does that entail? I've never actually thought about how they could do something like that."

"You may not *want* to know. It's pretty awful to think about. I'm terrified at the prospect. I haven't made up my mind yet if I can go through with it."

"I'm really interested."

"You're sure you want me to tell you?"

"Yes."

"Well, to put it simply . . . first they remove the testicles . . . then they . . . they cut the penis lengthwise . . . and then . . . they . . . core it out and cut off the glans."

"Jesus Christ!"

"Do you want me to go on?"

"Yes!"

"They sew it back up, turn it inside out, and invaginate it, if you will, up into the body cavity next to the rectum."

"That's unbelievable!"

"Ta-da! Instant pussy!"

"Is that it?"

"Well, they have to shorten and reposition the urethra . . . and then they form the labia majora with fatty tissue . . . but that's cosmetic . . . yes, that's basically it."

"God! You've got to *really want* to be a woman, don't you?"

Michael-Michelle just looked at Nathan for a moment. And then she began to cry softly.

"Yes," she said.

Nathan walked Michael-Michelle out to her car, which was parked in the lot behind The Cockpit. It was a brand new, powder blue Mercedes convertible.

"You must do pretty well at your photography business," said Nathan.

"I enjoy the work. I photograph beautiful women all day. What could be better for me?"

As Michael-Michelle unlocked her car, three thugs walked up to them aggressively, threateningly.

"Hey, faggot!" one of them said roughly. "Suck my dick!"

Nathan struck him hard in the mouth with his fist, then all hell broke loose.

When it was over, Nathan lay unconscious on the pavement with Michael-Michelle slumped over him, bleeding from the mouth and sobbing. The thugs had stolen her purse and fled. Nathan finally came to, picked Michael-Michelle up in his arms and placed her gently in the passenger seat of the Mercedes. He drove to the safety of her home, an apartment above the Michael Davidson Fashion Photography Studio in the heart of the Downtown Arts District.

Inside, they tended each other's wounds. Nathan cleansed Michael-Michelle's cut lips and helped her remove her bloodstained blue veil. She stood before him, nude and unashamed.

"Nathan, will you stay with me tonight?"

"I can't," said Nathan. "I . . . can't."

Michael-Michelle turned away and went to her bed. She lay face down, weeping softly. Nathan went over to her and sat on the edge of the bed.

"I like you," said Nathan. He put his hand tenderly on her back. "I want very much to be your friend. Can we just be friends?"

"Yes. I would like that, Nathan. I understand."

Nathan stood up to leave. He walked to the door and turned.

"Michelle . . . ."

"Yes?"

"You *are* a woman . . . to me."

Nathan took a bus back to Cedar Springs Avenue to pick up his car. By the time he returned to La Coterie, Lucinda was already sound asleep. He undressed quietly and slipped, nude, between the sheets. He snuggled up close against her satin-gowned body, drifted off into sleep, and dreamed sweet dreams of androgynous love.

FOURTEEN

When Nathan awoke, Lucinda was gone. She had left a note for him on the kitchen counter inviting him to stop by the gallery during the day to meet her new discovery, Vincent D'Amato.

Nathan ate breakfast, showered, and shaved (though, to his mild alarm, he didn't really need to). He dressed and left the condo. As he drove through the gate, he caught a glimpse of Baby Bow Wow chasing a much larger golden retriever around the corner of another pale yellow condo, identical to Lucinda's, near the high, iron security fence.

"Yahweh! Yahweh!" barked Baby Bow Wow.

Nathan stopped at a florist shop and bought a dozen white, long-stemmed roses. He had them boxed, wrapped in lavender paper, and finished off with a white satin ribbon tied into an elaborate bow. In an envelope taped to the outside, he placed a note: "For Michelle . . . my beautiful dancer . . . my beautiful friend." He drove to the Michael Davidson Fashion Photography Studio, parked, and went in the front door.

"Good morning," said a young, pretty woman seated behind a small reception desk. "May I help you?"

Nathan was taken aback. The large studio, which he could partially see over a low partition behind the receptionist, was a beehive of activity. Michael-Michelle, her long, blond hair in a no-nonsense ponytail, was all business. She was energetically moving about, snapping a handheld camera, stooping, kneeling, lying on the floor, standing on little ladders, busily photographing a strikingly elegant woman who was at least six feet tall.

Following Michael-Michelle closely as she weaved in and out among a forest of light stands were two female assistants holding additional cameras at the ready. A make-up artist, bristling with brushes, combs, and powder puffs, followed the action, occasionally darting into the frame to dab at the high cheekboned face of the model or to reposition an errant strand of her hair. The model, whose expression alternated between vacuousness and astonishment, changed poses quickly, subtly altering the position of her body or the attitude of her head in a series of stop-action, mechanical motions in contrapuntal rhythm to the clicking of the camera shutter. Her jerky movements reminded Nathan of the black transvestite voguers at The Lavender Ballroom.

"I'm here to see Michael Davidson," Nathan said to the receptionist.

"Michael's in session at the moment. Can you wait? He should be taking a break shortly."

"Yes. Thank you. I'll wait," said Nathan. He sat down on a powder blue leather sofa opposite the receptionist. On the walls were dozens of framed tearsheets from women's fashion magazines, presumably Michael-Michelle's published work. Most were clothing ads featuring glamorous models wearing everything from fur coats and jewelry to designer dresses to expensive silk lingerie. Mixed in among the ads were several extraordinarily sensuous black and white pictures of a young blond woman, photographed in every case so that her face was in deep shadow. In each picture, she seemed to be dancing, sheathed in wispy veils. Nathan, touched by a vague sadness, knew they were self-portraits.

"Nathan! What a surprise to see you!" said Michael-Michelle.

Nathan was also surprised, surprised to see her dressed in baggy pants, sweatshirt, and old tennis shoes. He stood up, and they awkwardly shook hands. Michael-Michelle looked just like a boy . . . a man. Nathan hardly recognized him.

"I . . . I hope I'm not interrupting," stammered Nathan, holding the box of roses behind his back.

"Not at all, Nathan!" said Michael-Michelle. His face was flushed with excitement, but Nathan wasn't sure if it was because of the unexpected visit or because of the highly active photo session he had just broken from. "Come on," said Michael-Michelle in a reasonably masculine voice. "Let's go in my office where we can talk."

Nathan followed him into the studio, between the lights and stands and tripods and over a rat's nest of electrical wires and cables, through a bustling group of people . . . assistants, make-up artist, wardrobe manager, art director, ad agency account executive, and models . . . all preparing for the next sequence of shots. Michael-Michelle showed Nathan into a small office behind the huge hanging sheets of seamless background paper and shut the door. He turned and looked at Nathan, hands on his hips, head cocked to one side, smiling flirtatiously.

"Now what are you hiding behind your back, big boy?" Suddenly she seemed just as feminine, despite her baggy clothes, as she had the night before.

"I . . . I . . . ." Nathan's face turned beet red with embarrassment. He wished he had not come.

"Come on," teased Michael-Michelle. "Show me what you have. Don't be shy."

"I guess this was a pretty stupid idea," said Nathan. He reluctantly handed her the box he had been trying to hide.

Michael-Michelle took the extravagantly wrapped present and looked up into Nathan's eyes, her expression now so serious she seemed about to burst into tears. "For me?" she asked in a whisper. She removed the envelope, started to open it, then placed it on her desk. She carefully unwrapped the box and slowly removed the lid. With a delicate touch of her dove-like hand she lightly caressed a single petal of one of the white roses. Her eyes, which she now kept averted from Nathan's, filled with tears. She put the box of flowers down on the desk and picked up the envelope. She opened it, removed the card, and read it.

"I didn't mean to . . . ." Nathan started to make some excuse for what he now thought was an overly mushy gesture of friendship that might be misinterpreted.

"I know what you meant, Nathan." Still holding the card, she came to him and embraced him. "Thank you," she said. "You are the sweetest man I have ever known. And I am honored to be your friend."

Michael-Michelle poured Nathan a cup of coffee, and they talked for the few minutes she had left before her next photo session. They talked mostly about Geronimo Jones, their mutual friend.

"I'm worried about him, Nathan. The big lug is so terribly vulnerable, you know. Lately he seems so unstable . . . almost schizophrenic. I'm afraid he might do something . . . something to hurt himself. He is totally unpredictable when he drinks."

"Yeah, I know," said Nathan. He told Michael-Michelle about the attack outside of La Coterie, about the drunken party that followed. Michael-Michelle knew all about Geronimo's Vietnam tragedy and about his obsessive search for Corporal Williams. But she evidently knew nothing about his new business venture with

Dr. Peter Smith, and Nathan decided not to spill the beans.

"Geronimo said you saved his life. What was he talking about? How did you save his life?"

"Oh, he's exaggerating. I . . . just lent him some money, that's all."

"Nathan, that was extremely kind of you, but you will probably never be repaid. Geronimo's income is practically zero . . . and what he does manage to earn he gives away to some religious freak he's involved with. That's something else I'm very worried about. Geronimo's lost touch with reality. I'm afraid of what he might do . . . to himself or to someone else. He could have *killed* you with that knife!"

"Don't worry about the religious freak," Nathan said. "I think I've talked Geronimo out of messing with him anymore. As far as his emotional problems . . . and his drinking . . . we'll just have to take care of him . . . you and me."

"Yes," she said, taking Nathan's hand. "We're the only friends he has."

"Michelle . . . what about these clothes you're wearing? I thought you said you always dressed as a woman."

"I do," she said, smiling mischievously. She raised her sweatshirt up to her chin, revealing a lacy pink chemise over a snugly fitting little satin brassiere. "I'm wearing a garter belt, silk hose, and lace panties, too."

"Wonderful!" said Nathan.

"I can't very well go around in a dress in front of my clients and my employees. I don't think they would understand, do you?"

"Probably not," said Nathan. He was blushing again, uncomfortably conscious of a maddening desire to fondle her budding breasts, to pull her baggy pants down and kiss her lacy, womanly buttocks. "I gotta go," Nathan said abruptly.

"When will I see you again?"

"I'll call you."

Nathan drove straight to Lucinda's gallery, five blocks away, dizzy with gender confusion. He concentrated on visualizing Lucinda's fabulous body, her full, smooth, tapering thighs, the way they parted so eagerly, so wantonly, in such grateful anticipation of his talented, phallic tongue; of her breasts, those intelligence-numbing, blood-boiling, astounding banana breasts, their little rosy faces upturned so expectantly, so . . . so . . . *fruitfully* . . . begging to he sucked . . . to be *nibbled*! Waiting at a stoplight, he tried to remember, precisely, exactly, the unique taste and texture of that darkening valley of skin at the tip of her spine where it plunged into the downy, humid cleavage of her Hottentot buttocks.

To his amazement and delight, Nathan felt his nearly-forgotten penis distend to full, bone-hard turgidity . . . his first complete erection, he happily noted, since his disastrous encounter with Baby Bow Wow. But, as usual, the intrusive thought of Baby Bow Wow and his sharp, cruel, little teeth caused him to wilt again, like a crocus in a late frost.

Nathan parked in front of the Dallas Gallery of Modern Art. A high brick wall surrounding the sculpture garden, where he and Lucinda had first met less than two weeks earlier, hid the gallery itself from view. Just ahead on the street was parked an old, beat-up Volkswagen bus. It was plastered with bumper stickers. One said: "Shit Happens!" Directly under it, another said: "Art Happens!" This has to be D'Amato's vehicle, thought Nathan sourly. He read on: "The World Sucks Art!" "Art Sucks The World!" This guy is definitely a nut, thought Nathan. But then he read three stickers in a row that he more or less had to agree with: "The Sun Hauls Ass" . . . "Truth Changes With Perspective" . . . and the most indisputable of claims, "Wherever You Go, There You Are."

Nathan got out of his Toyota and walked through the narrow gate in the garden wall, into the memory-charged stillness of Lucinda's erotic sculpture courtyard. He passed by the monstrous bronze statue of the nude woman, between whose muscular but softly rounded inner thighs he had first laid eyes on Lucinda. He ran his hand lightly over the statue's grotesquely exaggerated labia majora. The fat, dark, metallic lips felt cold as ice, despite the warm, sunny day. He followed the flagstone pathway, past the bench where Lucinda had sat eating her tuna fish sandwich, where he had first beheld those titillating tribal tits through the gap in her blouse. He rounded the quasi-cubist scrap metal representation of male genitalia, and again a shaft of sunlight struck and reflected from his thinning pate, only this time the light also cast an ever-so-slightly pear-shaped shadow of his body on the ground.

Nathan walked into the gallery where he found Lucinda poking through a huge pile of junk and trash in the middle of the floor. Through an archway to an adjoining room he could see another pile of junk, even larger, and a rather short, stocky, swarthy, shirtless man with a vigorous growth of black body hair sprouting from his back and shoulders. The man was energetically repainting Lucinda's bare, white walls a bright orange color. He sang as he worked . . . belting out an old Little Richard tune, "Good Golly Miss Molly." It was Vincent D'Amato, the mad genius from East Dallas.

"Lucinda!" Nathan called out over D'Amato's loud singing. Lucinda, startled by his voice, jumped and nearly fell back onto the pile of junk. He caught her by the arm.

"Oh, Nathan! I'm so glad you stopped by!" She was luminous with the glow that only great art or great sex can produce. "That's Vincent in there." She motioned to the squat Italian slinging orange paint and singing at the top of his lungs.

"I figured as much," said Nathan. "Orange? *Orange?*"

"Yes! Isn't it wild?!"

"What the hell's all this trash doing in here?"

"Those are Vincent's materials, Nathan. He is the most *incredible*, inventive, resourceful man I've ever seen! He's made two trips to the city dump already this morning!"

"Lucinda!"

"He's promised a complete transformation within a week . . . 'the apotheosis of garbage to ethereal art,' he calls it! He is so full of energy! So aggressive with *materials!*"

"Lucinda! Get a grip on yourself!"

"Nathan, you don't understand! That man . . . that man singing in there is one of the world's great artists! Do you know what he said to me? He said that the essence of civilization is in its garbage. That is a profound insight, Nathan! Vincent is reclaiming our souls, our cast off and forgotten essence. He is reclaiming it for us, recasting it, recombining it, and will, in his show, hold it up to us, like a mirror, so that the world can see itself as it truly is! Now *that* is art!"

"Bullshit, Lucinda! He's crazy! Look at your walls! Look at this stuff! *Look* at it! He's completely gone! Can't you see that? Can't you see that he's using your gallery to create a monument to his own madness?"

"He's *hot*, Nathan! Vincent D'Amato is . . . *will be* . . . hot in this town! And I've got him. I am singlehandedly organizing his first one-man show! I know what I'm doing! This will be a major happening! A pivotal art *event*!"

"Lucinda . . . please . . . I can't let you . . . ."

"This is my *thing*, Nathan! Don't get in my way!"

Lucinda and Nathan stared at each other for what seemed an eternity. D'Amato continued to sing and paint, unaware of their presence.

"You're sleeping with him, aren't you?" Nathan said finally.

Lucinda continued staring at him for a moment, unblinking. At last she answered, quietly, flatly.

"I wouldn't fuck Vincent even if I wanted to. He's completely unmanageable."

She turned on her heel, marched out of the room, and left Nathan, his anus cramping, standing amid the essence of civilization.

FIFTEEN

Nathan returned to La Coterie, angry, feeling helpless and afraid for Lucinda's well-being at the hands of the genius D'Amato. As he got out of his car under the gingerbread carport, he heard a terrific commotion in the tiny yard of a beige condo across the lane. At least two dogs were yelping and growling, and a woman was screaming and cursing. He ran toward the condo and looked over the polyvinyl chloride picket fence. Baby Bow Wow, hysterically snarling and snapping with fury, was butt to butt in coitus interruptus with the large golden retriever he had been chasing earlier in the day. A blue-haired old woman was beating them with a broom, trying to separate them.

Baby Bow Wow's penis, locked in the terrified retriever's contracted vagina, was bent back between his muscular little hind legs, which were absurdly elevated about four inches off the ground. He kicked and flailed the air with his dangling legs to no avail in his efforts to escape. As the screaming old woman beat at the dogs, the golden retriever ran frantically in circles, dragging Baby Bow Wow behind her on his front paws, often lifting him completely off the ground by centrifugal force. Nathan watched for a moment, relishing a delicious feeling of vicarious revenge, a most satisfying sense of schadenfreude.

Finally he took action, grabbed a hose from its hook on the side of the condo, and turned on the faucet. He sprayed the dogs with water, driving them into a frenzy of tangled, uncoordinated retreat.

At last Baby Bow Wow's little raw prick was somehow disengaged, and the retriever slinked whiningly over to the angry old woman who gathered the wet dog up protectively in her arms.

"You keep that nasty little mutt away from my Goldie!" screeched the old woman at Nathan. "He's violated every bitch on the block! He ought to be neutered!"

"I couldn't agree more!" said Nathan. He looked joyfully at Baby Bow Wow, who was running around in tight little circles, growling and snarling at his own penis, which, Nathan thought happily, must be sore as hell. He had once witnessed a dog with impacted bowels behave in a similar fashion years before in Virginia. That dog, who, like Baby Bow Wow, had been in considerable but (to him) inexplicable pain, had also run in circles, barking furiously at his own rectum.

Nathan went into Lucinda's condo and got a beer out of the refrigerator. He walked into the living room, turned on the TV, flipped the channel selector till he found Brother Larry Proffitt's Faith 'N Fortune show, then plopped down on the Early American sofa to watch once again and with renewed interest the outrageous antics of the most immoral pornographer, fornicator, and perverter of them all.

Presently, Baby Bow Wow came in through his little trap door in the kitchen. He trotted into the dining room, his little claws clicking on the polished hardwood floor, and took his spot under the table where he proceeded to lick his bruised and smarting genitals. Nathan watched him with extreme irritation.

Baby Bow Wow licked slowly, languidly, listlessly, his eyelids gradually drooping, his tongue making annoying little smacking sounds against his slobbering flews. Now and then he would look up when Brother Proffitt's voice would rise in pitch as he spoke in tongues, would watch him, possibly comprehending, Nathan thought, and would absently smack his mouth, over and over, as if sampling the unpleasant aftertaste of his swollen, slick little cock.

"Quo-dah-bah-sah-tah!" shouted Larry Proffitt, his snake-like eyes narrowing into slits of avarice and greed. "There's a pornicator out there right now, watching this show! You have sinned! *You* know you have sinned, Brother! *I* know you have sinned, and *God* knows you have sinned! You cannot hide from the Lord! REPENT NOW OR YOU WILL BURN IN HELL!!! Sow your seed of faith! Call the number on your screen right now and make your vow! God will forgive you, Brother. God will HEAL you! Ohhhh . . . Kashanda! Boh-tanda! CAST out the demons of FILTH! In the name of GEE-zus! Oh, YES, Lord! I FEEL your anointing ah-PONE me!"

"Listen up, Baby Bow Wow!" Nathan yelled. "Brother Larry is talking to YOU!"

"YAHWEH!" barked Baby Bow Wow.

Nathan, irked nearly to the breaking point, his anus starting to cramp up again, suddenly stood up, flipped off the TV, and stormed out of the condo. He got in his car and drove to the gate. Pops leaned out of the gatehouse window and called to him.

"Where you headed, Nathan?"

"Going to work off some steam, Pops!"

"Atta boy, Nathan!"

The gate slowly opened, and Nathan drove out and away from La Coterie, to his own quiet house in East Dallas, to the relative sanity of White Rock Lake.

At his house, Nathan changed into his riding shorts, worn-out denim jeans with the pant legs cut off. He urinated in a sample jar and locked it in his old salesman's briefcase . . . now his portable toilet, the essential accoutrement to his new career as manufacturer of testosterone-free urine.

Nathan rode his bicycle around the lake with a vengeance. Like the arrogant racers in their color-coordinated, skintight outfits, he startled unsuspecting strollers with silent, meteor-like close passes. He shot by the old lady with elephant skin and watery-blue eyes. She smiled at him vacantly as he passed. He acknowledged her with a nod. He sneered at a puffing middle-aged man, at his jiggling jowls, his bird-like legs, at the absurd and grotesque rictus of his oxygen-sucking mouth. He headed straight for the buxom redheaded girl, refused to yield, watched her veer, saw her cruise missile breasts bounce out of phase with her loping gait, watched her lose her balance and stumble.

"Asshole!" she said under her breath as he narrowly missed her.

Nathan tried to visualize her jogging in the nude, tried to imagine her moist, flame-red pubic hair glistening with perspiration in the bright sunlight, tried to picture her titanic tits bouncing out of sync al fresco. But somehow the vision would not come together. The vague fantasy vaporized as he approached a gaggle of coiffured, silly-walking, dumbbell-swinging housewives. Again he refused to yield, divided their ranks, ran them off on either side of the trail. He looked back over his shoulder, saw a fluorescent spandex rainbow of cellulite-dimpled fannies recede into the distance.

Nathan pedaled with abandon. It was the first time he had ridden his bike since his fateful loss to the hateful jaws of Baby Bow Wow. He noted with pleasure that the deucedly hard, narrow seat was not nearly so uncomfortable as it had been before, when his lone testicle had painfully bobbled from side to side over the diabolical horn of the saddle with the alternating thrusting of his thighs. He now fancied himself as riding with a new vigor and authority. He was, of course, unaware that from the back his body slightly resembled a pear perched on the thin little seat, which now nearly disappeared into the cleavage of his fattening nates.

Nathan stopped at a water fountain in a stand of old, gnarled black willow trees. He was breathless, hot, and drenched in sweat. He drank deeply, with his eyes closed. As he gulped the cool water, he sensed the presence of another warm, humid body near him. He looked up and saw the little girl . . . or woman . . . on roller skates. She, too, was breathless, waiting her turn to drink at the fountain.

"Hello," said Nathan.

She stared straight at him, piercing his soul with her steady gaze, and she smiled . . . that little enigmatic half-smile, innocent and yet infinitely wise. She did not speak. She went to the fountain and drank.

Nathan looked at her carefully. It was the first time he had had more than a mere glimpse of her. She wore blue denim cut-offs, as he did, and a sleeveless, pink cotton shirt. Her skates were the old-fashioned style, all metal, clamped onto the soles of her plain, brown leather shoes and secured to her pink-socked ankles with buckled straps. Nathan noticed that her knees were rough and scabby, but her skin was otherwise flawless, smooth, and tanned from the sun. Around her neck dangled a skate key on a frayed, pink ribbon; and a tonette . . . a simple black plastic flute . . . was tied to a rawhide thong, which she wore like a necklace. She stood up and wiped her lips with the back of her hand.

"My name is Nathan. What's yours?"

She didn't answer. She just stared at him, smiling. Nathan was struck by her mysterious beauty, by the way she stared at him so intensely, by the fact that she did not seem to mind him staring at her. He studied her face, her small body. Her eyes were green, deep-set, intelligent, and penetrating. Her tousled brown hair, damp with perspiration, was short and curly. Her breasts, still heaving from exertion, were small, and her nipples made two sharp little points under the soft fabric of her shirt. Her waist was slim, and her hips and her lean, muscular legs were those of a fully developed woman. But her unblemished face was that of a child.

"I've seen you skating around the lake many times," said Nathan. "I'm really glad to finally meet you."

She continued staring silently, just smiling at him.

To Nathan there was something very strange, almost mystical, about this woman-child. It seemed to him that, though she uttered not a word, she was somehow nevertheless communicating with him . . . on some level . . . and quite profoundly. He felt peaceful. At ease. Close to her.

"Do you live nearby?" he asked. When, again, she did not answer, he swept his arm in the direction of the houses along the shoreline and questioned with his eyes. She responded by raising her tonette to her lips and sounding three notes in ascending intervals, a simple triad of tones, but pure and clear and pregnant with significance. Her smile broadened, radiant with the joy of recognition. She turned and pointed to a rustic, cedar-shingled house ensconced in thick foliage and shaded by many large trees on the hill behind her. She looked back at Nathan.

Is that your house? Nathan surprised himself by asking the question silently. Again she played her flute, this time producing a long, sinuous, melodic line of notes, a kind of musical description, Nathan fancied, of her life, her dreams, her imaginings. He was enthralled, mesmerized. He felt he understood everything. And then suddenly she stopped playing as a pack of joggers approached, chuffing down the trail. She watched them pass, then looked back at Nathan.

"Can you speak?" Nathan asked. "Can you hear me?"

As she stared at him, her smile faded. She once again put the little plastic flute to her lips. But this time she played only two notes, portentous and haunting, the second note three whole-tones lower than the first. Though Nathan did not know its historical significance or its name, he understood the meaning of that universally baleful interval . . . the diminished fifth . . . the tritone . . . *Diabolus in musica* . . . a note pairing so evil-sounding that it was forbidden in early ecclesiastical music for eight centuries.

She turned and skated quickly away from him, down the path through the thicket of black willows, around a sharp bend, and out of sight. Nathan stood dumbly for a moment, then jumped on his bicycle and rode after her. He rounded the bend and scanned the long path twining through the trees, but she had vanished, as if into thin air.

Every day for the next two weeks, Nathan rode his bicycle around the lake, sometimes making two or three laps, looking for her. He spent hours loitering at the water fountain at the foot of the hill where her house stood, peering up into the dense shrubbery and trees that enshrouded it, trying to catch sight of her. One day he thought he saw her coming down the narrow stone walkway to the road, but it turned out to be an old man with white hair and a grave, ill face. As Nathan watched him limp down the hill to fetch his mail, he wondered if the man was her grandfather.

During those two weeks, prior to the opening of D'Amato's "pivotal" one-man show, Nathan spent the rest of his time reading, sailing, palling around with Geronimo and Michael-Michelle, and taking in the shows at The Lavender Ballroom. Lucinda was preoccupied with helping D'Amato set up his mirror to the world, apotheosizing garbage to art, sending out invitations, writing press releases, courting and teasing the art critics at the newspapers. They took her seriously. They knew her reputation. They considered her judgment infallible.

Lucinda and Nathan only occasionally made love during that period, and only on nights when he didn't go out with his friends who, according to Lucinda, were "too bizarre for words."

It seemed to take more and more effort to bring Lucinda to orgasm. One night, Nathan's tongue grew so tired it ached, and he had to stop. Lucinda rolled over on her stomach, put her hands between her legs, and masturbated while Nathan nuzzled her magnificent ass and massaged her quivering thighs. He never got another erection after the day he had fantasized about her while driving to her gallery, but it didn't seem to matter any more . . . to him or to Lucinda. He began to take long, solitary walks in the dark around the Arts District.

One day, about a week after he had lent the Kurt Vonnegut novels to old Pops MacDonald, Nathan stopped by the gatehouse to chat.

"So what do you think of Vonnegut, Pops? Did you read the books?"

"Yes, I did, Boy. And I liked 'em."

"Good."

"What do you think ol' Kurt's trying to tell us, Nathan?"

"To love one another, I guess. What do you think?"

"I think he's simply trying to tell us to stop hurting each other," said Pops. "And that doesn't necessarily mean we have to love each other. I think Vonnegut believes, as I do, that most all that ails us could be cured by a simple change in attitude."

"What kind of change in attitude?"

"Civility, Boy! Civility is nothing but an attitude . . . an attitude that can be learned. And *true* civility means courtesy, consideration, and kindness . . . most of all, kindness."

"And tolerance," said Nathan.

"No, I wouldn't say tolerance, Nathan. Tolerance implies a sense of superiority. I would say respect. Yes. I would add respect to courtesy, consideration, and kindness. That would do it."

"But that's not human nature, is it, Pops?"

"No, sadly for us, it's not. Most of us seem to naturally take on the attitude of all the damn dogs here at La Coterie: If you can't eat it or fuck it, then piss on it!"

"Yeah," said Nathan, thinking of Baby Bow Wow.

"And that's just plain selfishness, Nathan. That's really what's wrong with our society at bottom. We are a selfish people."

"You sound like a true Vonnegut fan, Pops. Want to read some more of his books? I've got at least a dozen more."

"Prolific bastard, wasn't he?"

"Still is. He just came out with a book of his memoirs. He's an old fart . . . nearly your age, I'd say."

"Yeah, bring 'em on, Nathan. I'll read 'em. Ain't got much else to do. Besides, I like reading books I agree with."

SIXTEEN

On the eve of Vincent D'Amato's epoch-making art event, Nathan asked for and received permission from Lucinda to invite his two "bizarre" new friends to the show opening.

"Just make sure they dress appropriately," Lucinda warned him. "I don't want them showing up in war paint and garter belts."

Nathan told Geronimo to wear his new suit, and he encouraged a reluctant, nervous Michael-Michelle to wear her prettiest party dress. "No one will ever recognize you," Nathan assured her. "It will be a good experience for you. Just think how feminine you'll feel making all the other women jealous."

The D'Amato show was to be Lucinda's most publicized art coup ever. She had done her groundwork well. Art critics and society columnists at the newspapers had already run special features and "personality" pieces on Lucinda and her gallery in anticipation of the show. They had wanted to do an article on D'Amato himself, but she had wisely kept him under wraps, creating an aura of mystery about him that only intensified everyone's curiosity.

She had allowed the *Dallas Times Herald* to print only one picture of D'Amato, in color, in the Sunday "ArtsWorld" section. It mainly showed a large expanse of bright orange wall divided into odd geometric sections by cryptic lines that D'Amato had drawn (or rather smeared) with some discarded oil sludge he had picked up at a gas station. In bas-relief within each section were what appeared to be fluffy gray clouds. They were actually old rags that

D'Amato, in a fit of spontaneous brilliance, had soaked in glue and thrown on the wall like giant spitballs. Where the sludge lines intersected, he had fastened to the wall various random samplings from the detritus of modern civilization: a smashed television, a worn-out radial tire, a half-eaten and smelly Egg McMuffin, a pair of ripped pantyhose, a cheap digital watch with a dead battery, a large empty roll-on deodorant bottle, and so forth and so on.

Squatting on the floor beneath this insightful work was the grinning, shirtless D'Amato, his dark, mysterious eyes blazing with artistic genius, his swarthy chest and shoulders bristling with hirsute virility.

The caption under the picture read as follows: "Vincent D'Amato with his *Essence In Orange*, one of the controversial works in his upcoming show at the *very* avant-garde Dallas Gallery of Modern Art." In an accompanying story, Lucinda was quoted as saying, "D'Amato is a genius. He picks up where Rauschenberg leaves off."

Lucinda had sent out five hundred engraved invitations to the cream of Dallas society. They were all rich. Some had made their fortunes fairly recently through their own efforts and cunning. A number of them had become wealthy by manipulating real estate before the bust. Others were wildly successful entrepreneurs in the artificial life extension industry. And at least five of those invited to the opening had retired on profits from theme restaurant franchise operations.

But many others, of course, had been smiled upon by God at their birth; they had been simply born into outrageously rich Texas families, families whose fortunes had been spawned in the good old days by cattle, cotton, oil, and cheap land. Unfortunately, a lot of those who had been blessed so early in life had grown up to be restless, confused, and unhappy because they had never known the satisfaction and fulfillment of useful work. They spent most of their time patronizing the arts and polishing their plaques of recognition and gratitude.

A few of the people Lucinda had invited, while rich, were actually on the fringe of Dallas' social elite; but she had sent them invitations anyway, because they were either good customers or special friends. Among them were Mrs. Thelma Pickett, art patroness extraordinaire and wife of West Texas wildcatter Bubba Pickett; Dr. Peter Smith, the urologist; and Brother Larry Proffitt. Brother Larry would not actually come, of course; a man in his unique position could visit her gallery only "incognito" for obvious reasons of propriety.

However, he had written a note to Lucinda in response, telling her that he was sending "a fine young man" in his stead, "a very talented and *serious* photographer" by the name of Eric Angstrom. He said in the note that he hoped Lucinda would "look at his photographs and consider showing his work at a future date." Lucinda would, of course, honor his request even though she knew it would be a waste of her time. Brother Larry had, after all, spent in excess of $75,000 at her gallery over the past two years on erotic sculpture.

On the night of the opening, Nathan picked up Geronimo and Michael-Michelle in his Toyota, and they all arrived at the gallery together. Geronimo was spiffed up in his new suit and a hand-painted Navajo necktie. He had found the tie in a Goodwill store. It had an interesting design in muted earthen colors, like an Indian sand painting, but it was at least twenty years old and was too wide to be fashionable.

Michael-Michelle, on the other hand, looked as if she had just stepped out of *Vogue* magazine. She was the epitome of style and femininity in her sleeveless blue silk dress, her delicate white shoulders caressed by her long blond hair, her daring décolletage accented by an exquisite pearl necklace. Her make-up was tasteful, subtle, and expertly applied . . . lip gloss, blusher, mascara, and light blue eye shadow. She stood four inches taller than usual in her coordinated blue kid high-heeled pumps, and her slender legs, shimmering in sheer blue matching stockings, whispered silkily, lightly brushing together as she walked. When she moved, Nathan could barely detect the faint outline of her garters and lace-trimmed panties under the liquefaction of her flowing dress. She was an absolute knockout.

Nathan, wearing one of his old salesman's suits, proudly escorted Michael-Michelle by her arm into the gallery, with Geronimo tagging behind.

D'Amato, looking . . . and walking . . . a bit like a disheveled, inebriated penguin in his ill-fitting rented tuxedo, greeted them obsequiously in the foyer. He had already hit the champagne, and he assumed they were rich.

"I am honored that you have come to witness my art," he said, bowing deeply. "Please, if you would be so kind . . . ." He led them to a guest register on a table opposite a portable bar that had been provided by the beverage caterer. The table and the bar were the only pieces of furniture in the gallery. Everything else had been stored in the basement to make room for the reclaimed and recombined waste of the great city of Dallas . . . "The City With No Limits," according to the Chamber of Commerce's latest self-promotion campaign.

They signed in, and D'Amato immediately put the move on Michael-Michelle.

"Come, my dear," he whispered in her ear. "Let me show you

the world through *my* eyes." He took her white dove-like hand in his hairy, thick genius hand and led her, with Nathan and Geronimo following, into the main gallery, a large interior space with a high cathedral ceiling.

Lucinda's gallery had, in fact, originally been a small Baptist church, built in 1925. When the congregation suddenly increased dramatically in the early eighties with the arrival of a new charismatic pastor who spoke to them in tongues, they were forced to move to North Dallas and build a larger facility. Lucinda bought the abandoned church and remodeled it, leaving the choir balcony at one end of the sanctuary for atmosphere.

D'Amato's show, Nathan noted with a smirk, was just what he had expected: a hellish orange nightmare of meaningless junk and garbage. The centerpiece, "Essence in Orange," was even more overwhelming, offensive, and perplexing than it had appeared to be in the newspaper picture. It covered an entire wall, from one end of the gallery to the other, and was twelve feet in height, reaching up as high as the old choir balcony on the adjacent wall. The other walls were basically orange, too, but had been over-painted with various dubious substances in the apparently haphazard, spontaneous, "action" style of, say, Jackson Pollock. The entire gallery appeared to have been vandalized.

Placed here and there on the floor were roughly a dozen "constructions," soaring "recombinations" of every conceivable worthless object . . . everything from mangled fenders and bumpers off wrecked cars, to desiccated food and other more questionable organic matter, to broken toys and household appliances . . . all juxtaposed willy-nilly in a contrary if not insane incongruity. Each "sculpture" bore a title at its base. One was dubbed "Evolution in Rust." D'Amato called another "The Disease of Culture." Et cetera, et cetera.

One particularly odious stroke of D'Amato's genius was manifested in a kind of shadow box affair, hermetically sealed in clear acrylic, which lay flat on the floor. The box, lined in rabbit fur, contained an artful arrangement of animal parts that he had secured from the local abattoir. In the center was a dead domestic cat. With the typical mordant irony of certain self-important artists who are forever trying to explain the inexplicableness of their work, he had named the inspired piece: "What Is It About Animals That Charms Us So?"

Good question, thought Nathan as he looked closely at the cat, trying to decide if it was stuffed. He tried to visualize Baby Bow Wow in its place.

"Oh, Vincent! There you are!" It was Lucinda, dressed to kill in basic black, the high priestess of Dallas art. She had a large, rawboned, peroxide-blond woman in tow who was wearing a $15,000 Paris original and a king's ransom in jewelry. "Vincent, I want you to meet Thelma Pickett. She's come all the way from Lubbock just to see your show!"

D'Amato bowed deeply. "I am honored that you have come to witness my art," he said again. Nathan was certain he had been coached by Lucinda.

"Wal dang my hide!" said Thelma. "I'm mighty glad to be here! I ain't never seen such highfalutin art!"

"You are too kind, madame," said D'Amato, bowing again. "I am only a humble man trying to create a kinder, gentler world through my art."

"Wal if that don't beat all! I shore wish Bubba was here to see this! He'd have a conniption fit!"

"Bubba is Thelma's husband," Lucinda explained. "He's in the oil business in West Texas." As she spoke, she was looking hard at Michael-Michelle, examining every detail of her attire. Michael-Michelle pretended not to notice. Lucinda finally shifted her gaze to Geronimo, briefly studied his unusual tie, then looked at Nathan with an expression in her eyes that he had never seen before and could not fathom.

"Say, how much you wantin' for that little ol' statue over there with the toaster on top?" Thelma asked D'Amato.

"Domestic Miasma?" D'Amato gave the title of the piece he thought she was referring to. He looked at Lucinda for guidance.

"That particular piece is perhaps Vincent's finest work," Lucinda said to Thelma. Her voice was suddenly all business. "I would purchase it myself as an investment if I could afford it. It will *definitely* triple in value within two years. 'Domestic Miasma' is currently available for $12,500."

D'Amato's mouth fell open. Michael-Michelle played it cool. Geronimo didn't understand. Nathan said "shit" under his breath. Lucinda shot him a look that would have withered his balls if he'd had any.

"Hell, I done paid more 'an that for this goosey dress!" exclaimed Thelma. "I'll take it!"

"I'll have it delivered," said Lucinda. She quickly took Thelma by the arm to lead her into the gallery office to close the deal and get her check. As she left, she gave Nathan another look over her shoulder. He couldn't decide whether it was a look of anger, warning, jealousy, or sadness.

D'Amato's opening was a ripping financial success. When the word got out that Thelma Pickett had purchased "Domestic Miasma" (and Lucinda made sure that it did), the crowd of wealthy, aesthetically insecure art connoisseurs went into a feeding frenzy. Up to that point, they had not really looked at D'Amato's work, their primary objective being to see and be seen themselves. But that objective quickly switched to one of social one-upsmanship, to a competitive game of cultural status-seeking in which the contestant paying the most outrageous price for something too hideous to behold became the winner.

Lucinda was so busy in her office writing up orders that she missed the best part of the show . . . the most significant and inspired "performance-art" statement ever made by Vincent D'Amato.

Late in the evening when only Lucinda's friends and the most hard-core social climbers and sycophants were still present, when nearly everyone was well over the line with champagne, D'Amato appeared buck naked on the choir balcony.

"The whole world SUCKS!" screamed D'Amato. "PISS ON IT!!" Whereupon, he proceeded to urinate on his intimidating and disturbing "Essence In Orange" from above, sprinkling its intricate web of sludge sections, its spitball clouds, and its bitter symbols of modern civilization. "The world is my art! My art is the world!" he shouted. "When I piss on my art, I piss on the world! Join me, my friends! PISS WITH ME!!"

Two or three people left in disgust. Most simply backed away a safe distance from "Essence In Orange" and watched the fun. A surprising number of men actually whipped out their tallywhackers and urinated on the works they had found most obnoxious.

Nathan and Geronimo started to unzip their flies, too, but they were brought up short by their employer, Dr. Peter Smith, who had alertly moved up behind them. He placed his cold, greedy, entrepreneur hands firmly on their shoulders.

"You take a leak in here, and I'll dock you," he said quietly.

Nathan and Geronimo both looked around nervously to see if Michael-Michelle had heard what Smith had said, but she was nowhere to be seen. They went to find her.

As they left the gallery, Nathan saw a young woman with a punk hairdo squatting over the brilliantly ironic D'Amato work that asked the probing question, "What Is It About Animals That Charms Us So?"

They finally found Michael-Michelle out in the sculpture garden. She was sitting on a bench chatting with Eric Angstrom, the "*serious*" art photographer sent by Brother Larry Proffitt. They had left the gallery, together, when D'Amato had started pissing on the world.

"Eric, these are my dear friends, Nathan Doering and Geronimo Jones," said Michael-Michelle.

"Hello," said Eric. He stood up and shook their hands. "I'm Eric Angstrom," he said solemnly. He was a tall, handsome young man with shoulder-length red hair. His face, bearded and with tortured eyes that seemed to express the full sorrow of the world, strongly resembled the haunting face of Jesus Christ that Nathan had seen and been terrified by on the back of a fan in church when he was a child.

"What do you think of D'Amato's work?" Nathan asked him.

"I think it is pretentious, hysterical, and intellectually dishonest," said Angstrom. "D'Amato is missing the point entirely."

"What *is* the point?" Nathan pressed on. There was something about Angstrom's lugubrious seriousness that annoyed him.

"The point is . . . is that life is absurd. Existence itself is absurd. What we call civilization is the ultimate absurdity, and it is naive and inappropriate to rail on about it as D'Amato does. That angry young man shit went out in the sixties. The only intelligent and sane

response to an absurd universe in the nineties is quiet contemplation
. . . or indifference . . . or suicide. That is the point."

"Excuse me," said Nathan, "but I think your *nihilistic* young man
shit went out in the fifties."

"Get a life! I'm talking *neo*-nihilism here!"

"Whatever," said Nathan. He realized he was getting in over his
head. "Why can't everybody just relax and try to have a good time?"

"I'm with you, Kemosabi!" said Geronimo. Geronimo didn't like
to think about suicide. His mother had killed herself when he was
ten years old. Dying in a nursing home of emphysema from smoking
a pipe all her life, she had intentionally flicked her Bic in her oxygen
tent and had blown herself up to the happy hunting grounds.

The conversation with Eric Angstrom essentially ended at that
point. Nathan drove Michael-Michelle and Geronimo home and
went back to La Coterie. He waited up until Lucinda came home at
four a.m.

"What kept you so long?" Nathan asked sleepily.

"I've discovered a brilliant new artist, Nathan! His work is
absolutely *incredible*! And he came to me out of nowhere!"

"Let me guess," said Nathan. "A neo-nihilist photographer who
looks like Jesus Christ."

"How did you know?"

SEVENTEEN

Nathan lay sprawled in the cockpit of his sailboat, becalmed in the middle of White Rock Lake. In his left hand he held his fifth can of beer since setting off an hour before. In his right hand he cradled and absently twiddled his scrotum, which dangled lifeless and empty from the gap in the crotch of his cut-off jeans. He was thinking about his life . . . trying to sum things up. He felt confused and depressed.

I'm not only castrated physically, he thought glumly, I'm castrated emotionally, intellectually, and spiritually. He thought about suicide and wondered what it would feel like to be indifferent to the universe. Unable to imagine such a peaceful state, he finished his beer and drifted off to sleep, unaware of the rapidly gathering thunderheads in the southeastern sky.

A flash of lightning and a crack of thunder woke him from his drunken slumber. The wind came up quickly, rising in sharp gusts. The boat pitched and rolled on the frothing whitecaps, and the boom swung dangerously from side to side. Nathan scrambled clumsily to lower the sails and stow them in the tiny forepeak. He had no anchor; all he could do was ride with the howling wind and try to keep his little boat from capsizing. In the darkening yellow-green light of the sudden squall, the clouds roiled angrily, and rain slanted down in cold, fat dollops, stinging his face. As his boat was blown closer and closer to the northwestern shore, Nathan realized that he would surely hit the rocks along the bank. There was nothing he could do to prevent it. He braced himself.

Over the sounds of screaming wind, crashing thunder, and waves breaking on unseen rocks, he heard the sickening crunch of rending fiberglass as the fragile hull slammed against the shore, throwing him forward on impact. He saw one last, bright flash of lightning as his head struck the aluminum mast with a loud bong.

When Nathan regained consciousness, he was warm and dry. He was dressed in strange clothes and was lying on an unfamiliar bed in a semi-darkened room. An old white-haired man with a grave, ill face was sitting in a chair by the bed, bending over him, gently slapping his cheek.

"Come on, Boy. That's it . . . that's it," said the old man in a raspy voice. "Wake up now . . . come on . . . that's it."

"Stop hitting me," said Nathan irritably. "My head is killing me." He felt the top of his head. It was bandaged, and it was sore. "Where am I?" he asked the man. "Who are you?"

"My name is Moses Weisman," he said. "You are safe in my home. Violet saved your life."

"Violet?"

Moses pointed an arthritic finger to a corner of the room. There in the shadows sat the mysterious woman-child. She was staring at them. In the dim light from the curtained windows, Nathan could not tell if she was smiling.

"Violet found you," said Moses. "She dragged you from the rocks, then came and got me. We carried you up here. You're lucky to be alive. You smell like a brewery. You should know better than to drink when you're boating. What's your name?"

"Nathan Doering."

Nathan looked over at Violet. "Thank you," he said to her.

"My daughter can't hear you," said Moses. "She's deaf."

"I'm sorry," said Nathan.

"Don't be sorry, Boy. It's a blessing."

"How can deafness be a blessing?"

Moses looked sadly into Nathan's eyes for a moment, then shifted his gaze to his own gnarled, crippled hands resting on the edge of the bed. Nathan could hear his lungs rattling and whistling with phlegm as he labored to breathe.

"Perhaps I'll try to explain sometime," he said finally. "Right now you should try to rest for a while. Dinner will be ready in an hour. I hope you'll join us."

"Thank you," said Nathan. "That's very kind of you."

Moses stood and started to leave, then turned back and looked at Nathan. "Violet seems to be fond of you. How do you know her?"

"I don't. I've only seen her skating around the lake . . . and I tried to talk to her once. She played her flute for me. I felt like she was trying to . . . to talk to me that way."

"Ah," Moses smiled. "And did you understand what she was saying?"

"Yes . . . in a way . . . I think I did."

"Good," said Moses. "See you at the table later. We'll talk." He left the room.

Nathan looked over again at Violet. She was still staring at him. He motioned for her to come, and she tentatively stood up and walked over to his bed. He formed a silent thought of thanks and tried to project it with his eyes. Violet smiled and raised her tonette to her lips. She gave Nathan a soft, breathy B-flat, then tenderly touched his forehead with her fingertips.

At dinner, Moses directed the conversation, keeping it to small talk. He had Nathan tell him about his house across the lake, about his cycling and sailing. He informed Nathan that his sailboat had sunk just offshore, that only the top few inches of its mast were visible above the water. He told him again that he should consider himself lucky to be alive after being caught, drunk as he was, in a storm like that. And he pointed out again, proudly, that Violet had saved his life.

All through the meal, which Moses had prepared himself, Nathan and Violet mostly stared at each other. He tried to guess her age, wondered if she were as old as his daughter Rose would be by now. He felt peaceful and close to her, as he had that day at the fountain. He tried to imagine what Rose would look like, imagined that she might look a lot like Violet.

When they were finished eating, Moses patted his hand on the table; Violet, apparently feeling the vibration, turned her gaze from Nathan and looked at her father. Moses smiled at her and nodded. As if responding to a silent command, she got up from the table, came over and kissed her father, and left the room.

Moses went into the kitchen and came back with a pot of coffee and two cups. He sat down and poured some for himself.

"Want coffee?" he asked.

"Thanks," said Nathan. "Mr. Weisman, I . . . ."

"Call me Moses," he said, filling Nathan's cup.

"Moses . . . will you tell me what you meant by Violet's deafness being a blessing?"

Moses stirred his coffee, watched the spoon make a steaming vortex in his cup.

"When I removed your wet clothes," he said, "I couldn't help noticing the scars on your scrotum. You appear to have no testicles.

Am I right?"

Nathan was astonished at this non sequitur, but he answered his question. "Yes. That's right. I've been castrated. But what's that got to do with Violet's deafness?"

"Nothing. I don't want to talk about that now. I want to know about you. How did it happen?"

Nathan told Moses about the horrible loss of his manhood in Lucinda's bedroom, how Baby Bow Wow had even swallowed his one and only testicle and then spit it up, and how the sight of his ball lying on the hooked rug had caused him to pass out.

Moses howled with laughter, which made him wheeze and gasp for air. Nathan grew concerned when he began to cough violently and uncontrollably, nearly falling out of his chair. Finally Moses settled down and wiped the tears from his eyes with a table napkin.

"I'm glad you find my misfortune so amusing," Nathan said, more amazed at his reaction than offended by it.

"I'm not laughing at your misfortune, Boy. It's the way it happened that's so funny. Surely you can see the humor in it."

"Frankly, no, I can't. There's nothing funny about that dog, believe me."

"I hope you will be able to laugh about it someday, Nathan. A life without humor and whimsy, without the ability to make something good come out of your own grief, is not worth living."

Moses questioned him closely, skillfully, relentlessly. Nathan wound up telling him his life story. Moses seemed particularly interested in hearing about his baby daughter Rose, made him talk about his sorrow.

Then Nathan turned the tables.

"You are very ill, aren't you?" he asked.

"Oh, I have a touch of emphysema," said Moses. "And I'm dying of lung cancer. I'll be gone in two or three months."

"I'm sorry," said Nathan.

"Quit saying you're sorry about everything, Boy! *I'm* not sorry. I'm an old man. I've had a good life. An interesting life."

"Tell me about it," Nathan said. "It's your turn."

Moses told Nathan about his early youth as a Jew in pre-war Germany. He said he remembered that the sun was always shining in those days. And then the darkness of Hitler fell. His parents and his sister were murdered in the streets of Munich, and he was taken to a concentration camp. There he met Anna, his future wife. Together they had miraculously survived the horror and privation of the camp and had come to America after the war.

"In New York we learned to dance, Nathan. It helped us to forget. We were good together. We went on the road professionally, and we made a good living. We toured the world, dancing ourselves into oblivion."

Moses stopped talking and closed his eyes. He was silent for a long moment. Nathan wanted to say he was sorry again, but he didn't.

"Our big mistake, Nathan, was that we stopped dancing. We came to Dallas and settled down. Oh, we still danced, but not like before. We missed the gaiety, the whirl and distraction of travel and exotic places. We had too much time on our hands."

"Why on earth did you decide to settle in Dallas?" Nathan asked. "Of all the beautiful places in the world you could have gone, why this cheerless city?"

"It didn't seem so bad at the time. And I found this property on the lake. I wanted to build a house with my own hands. Anna and I opened a dance studio in town. We taught hundreds of people how to dance. We changed people's lives, Nathan. We had a good time.

We were happy for a while."

Nathan saw Moses' old eyes tear up as he shakily poured them more coffee.

"What happened?" Nathan asked.

"Everything changed when Violet was born. When we discovered she was . . . was not normal, Anna began to drift away from both of us into her own private world. It was her way of dealing with the unbearable pain of her memories . . . with the grief she felt over Violet. She began to write poetry. That was what killed her, Nathan. The words killed her. She stopped dancing and gave into the tyranny of words. I found her in her little greenhouse out back one day, lying in a bed of violets she had planted. She had closed the vents and turned on the gas."

They both sipped their coffee in silence for a long while. Nathan felt unnatural not offering his condolences.

"What happened with the dance studio?" Nathan finally asked. "Did you continue dancing?"

"I converted the studio into a nightclub, a place for people to dance away their sorrow when they couldn't sleep. And, yes, I continued teaching people *how* to dance . . . up until a few years ago when my health began to fail. The club is still going strong. It's changed over the years, though."

"You still own it?"

"Yes. It's called The Cockpit now. There's still a beautiful ballroom upstairs. But it's mainly for homosexuals these days."

"You own The Cockpit?! The Lavender Ballroom?!" Nathan was flabbergasted.

"You know the place, Boy?"

"My best friends work there! Geronimo Jones and Michael Davidson!"

"Ah! Michael-Michelle! A *fine* dancer! The best! Have trouble remembering she's really a boy, though."

"Moses, I'm really surprised that you would own a homosexual bar."

"It just evolved that way, Nathan. The boys started coming in gradually at first. After a while it became their place. And I was glad to see it happen. I encouraged it."

"Why?"

"Homosexuals in America are a persecuted and disenfranchised people, Nathan, much like the Jews in Nazi Germany. They need a place where they can meet in peace and relative safety. They need a place to dance, too. Are you homosexual, Boy?"

"No, I'm not," said Nathan. "But sometimes I think my life might have turned out better if I could have . . . could have been that way."

"How did you come to know Michael-Michelle?"

Nathan told him how Geronimo had introduced them at the Lavender Ballroom. Moses listened sadly to the story of how Geronimo had attacked Nathan in the Arts District, thinking he was Corporal Williams, how they had talked into the night, and how Nathan had befriended him. Moses knew Geronimo well. He had hired him at The Cockpit after the Vietnam War when no one else would give him a job. But he was not aware that Geronimo was still obsessed with finding Corporal Williams, and he knew nothing of his enslavement to the false hope of the Faith 'N Fortune racket.

"That Proffitt is a truly evil man," said Moses. "He needs to be stopped. In a way, he's more dangerous than Hitler. At least Hitler never pretended to be working for God."

Nathan decided to tell Moses how he had helped Geronimo by introducing him to Dr. Peter Smith. He told him the whole bizarre story of the *Pierre: For Men* venture. Moses listened in amused astonishment until Nathan, not thinking, mentioned Skinner's involvement.

"Damn that boy! He doesn't know when to stop with his greed!" exclaimed Moses.

"I'm sorry," said Nathan. "I didn't mean to get him in trouble. I forgot he works for you."

"He's my son," said Moses.

"Your son?! But . . . his name is Skinner! I don't understand."

"He took his mother's name. He's ashamed of being a Jew."

"I still don't understand."

"After Anna died, I took on a housekeeper. Someone to look after Violet. I was lonely. She got pregnant, gave birth to Jacob, and then ran off, leaving him with me. I raised him . . . and Violet . . . by myself."

"J for Jacob," said Nathan. "As in J. Charleton Skinner, III."

"The 'Charleton' and that 'third' business, he made that up. His name was Jacob Weisman until he graduated from law school. He thought being a Jew in Dallas would hold him back. He was probably right. But Jacob never understood what's really important in life."

"So . . . so he manages The Cockpit for you. You're still close."

"I wouldn't call it close. He's just waiting for me to die, and he won't give Violet the time of day. But he's still my son. I still love him."

"But . . . if he was born after Violet . . . that would make him younger . . . . Moses, how old *is* Violet?"

"She's thirty-six. Doesn't look it, does she, Boy?"

"I can't believe it! She looks almost like a child!"

"Violet *is* a child, Nathan. And that's very important for you to understand. She has the body of a grown woman, but mentally and emotionally . . . and *sexually* . . . she simply stopped developing when she was three years old. Do you understand what I'm saying?"

"Yes . . . I think I do. I hope you don't think . . . ."

"Look, I've seen you hanging around in front of the house for the past two weeks. I've seen you and Violet just staring at each other here at the table. I'm not sure of the nature of your attraction to her, but you *must* understand that any sexual activity would be unnatural and psychologically damaging to her. Is that absolutely clear? It would be nothing short of child abuse."

"Moses, I *assure* you that I have no sexual interest in Violet. I don't fully understand my attraction to her either, but I *am* very strongly drawn to her. My feeling for her is . . . I would . . . almost call it paternal. In a way, she reminds me of my own daughter."

"That's good, Nathan. I'm very happy to hear you say that. Violet needs a friend like you . . . someone she can communicate with . . . someone sensitive enough to understand her special language. And I think you *do* understand . . . or at least I think you have the potential to understand."

"Language?"

"Yes, it *is* a language . . . of sorts. Over the years, we have developed a kind of musical method of communication. Not melodic, really . . . more a contextual combination of intervals. It can become quite complex and expressive sometimes. It's really more a language of feelings rather than of ideas or things."

"But I thought you said Violet is deaf."

"She is. Stone deaf. And mute. When we talk, so to speak, I play the piano . . . I improvise my feelings, suggest my thoughts. She feels the vibrations of the notes with her hand on the piano. She responds by playing her little flute. She can hear herself through the vibrations on her fingertips."

"That's extraordinary!"

"Yes! Extraordinary and wonderful! It's not as precise as the spoken word, of course. But in some ways, very important ways, it is a far better language than speech. Words are slippery, tricky things, Nathan. In human relationships, I have an idea that words hurt more than they help. It's too easy to be dishonest with words. But music is pure. It is what it is. Music does not lie."

Nathan recalled how Violet had charmed him that day at the fountain, the way the simple notes she played on her flute had seemed to speak to him. And then he remembered the evil-sounding pair of notes she had sounded just before she skated away from him so hurriedly. He told Moses about that.

"Oh, yes," he laughed. "That's Violet's way of expressing anger. She doesn't like you to talk to her. Once you start speaking, communication stops."

"But, Moses, I know so little about music. I don't play the piano."

"You don't need to be a musician, Nathan. All you need to do is play notes and create intervals as you feel them. Come, I'll show you."

He led Nathan into the living room. Violet was sitting on the sofa, turning the pages of a *National Geographic* magazine.

"Can she read?" Nathan asked Moses.

"Of course not! She's three years old! Remember?"

Moses sat down at the piano and looked over at Violet. She put the magazine down and came over to the piano, placing her hand lightly on the soundboard. Moses began to play. He played a long succession of notes . . . no recognizable melody . . . no particular rhythm . . . sustaining some of them . . . playing others staccato . . . a wistful, heartfelt line of notes that Nathan found sublimely simple and beautiful. Then he stopped, and Violet raised her tonette to her lips. She played as she had played the day she and Nathan had met at the fountain. She looked back and forth from her father to Nathan as she played, watching their faces intently. Then she stopped, stared at Nathan, transfixed him with her smile.

"She likes you, Nathan," said Moses. "Come. Play something for her."

"I can't . . . I don't . . . ."

"Try, Nathan. Just play what you feel."

Nathan sat down on the piano bench next to Moses. He hesitantly pressed a key. Then another. Then several more.

"That's not what I wanted to play," he said. "I don't know where the notes are. I really should go now." He stood up to leave.

"I'll teach you, Nathan. You can come here anytime," said Moses. "Let me help you. It would mean a great deal to Violet."

Nathan looked at Violet. She played one clear note on her flute that seemed to affirm what her father had said.

He agreed to return the next day for a music lesson.

Nathan walked five miles in the dark around the north end of the lake to his car where he had parked it at the boat club. Still wearing the dry clothes in which Moses had dressed him, he drove back to La Coterie, to a world that now seemed distant and strange and dangerous.

EIGHTEEN

The next morning, Nathan drove back to the lake and stopped on the road in front of the Weisman house. He got out and walked to the edge of the rocks on which he had foundered in the squall the day before. Just offshore he could see the top of his boat's mast sticking up out of the water. He considered the possibility of salvaging the boat and having it repaired, but he calculated that it would cost more than the boat was worth. He decided to forget it.

He got back in his car and turned into the Weisman's driveway, wound his way up the hill through the shady trees and parked at the side of the house. As he got out, he heard a screen door slam, looked up and saw Violet running out to greet him. She threw her arms around his neck like a child and kissed him on the cheek. She took his hand and led him into the cool, dark house that her father had built with his own hands. Inside the house, Nathan felt happy and peaceful. He felt at home.

Moses was sitting in an easy chair by a window in the living room. He was holding a newspaper close to his face, squinting at it through a large magnifying glass. As Nathan and Violet entered the room, he peered up over the paper.

"Good morning, Nathan. I'm glad to see you," he said. Moses did not look well. He coughed, putting his fist to his mouth, holding it there with his eyes closed, breathing through his nose.

"Are you all right?" Nathan asked.

"Ah . . . I have good days, and I have bad days, Nathan. This is not such a good day."

"Can I get you anything? Have you had breakfast?"

"I'm fine, Son. Thank you." He looked back through his glass at the paper. "Say, listen to this, Nathan. It says here that a new book on how to commit suicide has hit the bestseller list. Can you imagine that? Who would want to read a book like that?"

"Neo-nihilists."

"What?"

"I don't know, Moses. It wouldn't interest me."

"Me neither, Nathan. I don't care how much pain I'm in. I want to live every last minute I can."

He coughed again, his old lungs wheezing and rattling. Nathan watched him sadly.

"Do you read the newspaper, Son?"

"Rarely," said Nathan. "It's too depressing."

"Do you read books?"

"Yes."

"What sort of books?"

"Novels, mostly. Have you ever read anything by Kurt Vonnegut?"

"Kurt Vonnegut . . . . Is he a Nazi?"

"No," Nathan laughed. "He was a *prisoner* of the Nazis. He survived the fire bombing of Dresden. He's an American novelist. A great writer."

"Can't say I've heard of him. I don't read that much anymore. Never did read fiction anyway."

"Why not?"

"Fiction's too dull compared to what goes on in real life." Moses put his paper and magnifying glass down on a side table and stood up slowly. "Come on, Son. Let me show you how easy it is to play the piano."

Moses showed Nathan how to play scales.

"This is all you need to know to talk to Violet," he said. "Practice your scales backwards and forwards until you know the entire keyboard by heart. Pretty soon, if you practice hard, you'll be able to play any note in your head without thinking about where it is on the piano. Then you can look at her while you play. That's important. Half the communication is in the eyes, you see."

"Yes. I've noticed that. Thank you, Moses. Shall I practice now?"

"Feel free to stay as long as you like, Son. You're always welcome here. I'm going to lie down now for a bit."

Moses and Violet left the room and shut the door. Nathan practiced his scales for two hours. At noon they all ate lunch together, after which Nathan washed the dishes while Violet dried. Moses retired again to his bed, and Nathan took Violet for a long walk around the neighborhood. Later in the day, Moses was feeling better, and he and Nathan talked until dinner time while Violet tirelessly turned the pages of magazines, looking at pictures. Nathan insisted on preparing dinner, and Moses let him. After the meal, Nathan practiced his scales again. He left the house only after Violet went to bed at eight o'clock.

Driving back to La Coterie, Nathan could not recollect ever having spent a more pleasant day in his life.

When Nathan walked into the condo, Lucinda was sitting in the middle of the living room floor, poring over mountains of photographs stacked all around her. It was the prodigious work of the neo-nihilist Eric Angstrom.

"Hello. What's this?" Nathan said in a chipper voice.

"Nathan! Look at these photographs!" Lucinda exclaimed. "Just *look* at them! They are absolutely *incredible*!"

Nathan looked. Not one of them contained an image. They were all blank.

"They're all blank," Nathan stated matter-of-factly.

"Well, yes . . . and no," said Lucinda.

"What do you mean, 'yes and no'? They are definitely blank."

"That's the point, Nathan. The fact that they are blank communicates a significant message. What Eric is saying here is that, ultimately, all is nothing. I think they are *incredibly* powerful in their austere simplicity."

"That's very interesting, Lucinda. Have you eaten yet?"

"I mean, look at *this* one, Nathan!" She held up a large, light grayish-toned print. "Isn't it *magnificent?*"

Nathan looked at the print thoughtfully.

"I saw fog like that once on the Chesapeake Bay," he said truthfully. "I was fishing with my daddy. I couldn't see my hand in front of my face. At first I felt scared, but then my daddy put his arm around me and held me, and then I felt safe and peaceful. I like fog."

"What the hell are you talking about?"

"How much does Eric want for that one, Lucinda? If it's under $12,500, I might consider buying it."

"O.K., Mr. Smartypants. You made your point. So what *does* it take to please you? What do *you* consider good art?"

"I like art that makes me feel good," said Nathan. "And it's all right if it makes me sad, because you have to be sad some of the time if you're ever going to be happy. But, at least, art should *affirm* life, not tear it down. I can *read* about how rotten the world is in the newspapers, if I want to rub my nose in it. And I can learn all I want to know about the sickness of our society just by walking down the street. I don't need D'Amato to tell me how ugly I am, and I certainly don't need Eric Angstrom to tell me how absurd I am."

Lucinda, either unable to think of something pertinent to say, or more likely, thinking it best not to say anything, looked back at the photographs on the floor, stared silently into the infinite nothingness of Angstrom's soul.

"I'm sorry, Lucinda. I didn't mean anything personal. To each his own, right? I mean, what do I know about art? I'm just an ignorant high school drop-out. I have no business passing judgment on such things."

"You may be ignorant, Nathan, but you're not stupid. You have a valid point of view, and you have every right to express it. I just don't happen to agree with you. But I still like you. A lot."

Lucinda stood up and hugged Nathan.

"Come on," she said. "Let me fix you something to eat."

"I've already had supper."

"Well, then, let's go to bed."

Who needs *Pierre: For Men?* thought Nathan as Lucinda led him by the hand up the stairs to her bedroom. Art, not urine, is the world's most powerful aphrodisiac.

In the waterbed, Nathan tried hard to give Lucinda an orgasm. He wasn't especially aroused himself, but he wanted very much to please her. His libido might be slipping a little, he thought, but his technique was as brilliant as ever. For the art of cunnilingus was like the art of riding a bicycle . . . once you got the knack, you never forgot how to do it.

However, Lucinda lost interest before he did. She didn't even want to masturbate. She wanted to talk.

"What have you been doing today?" she asked. "Whose clothes were you wearing when you came in last night?"

Nathan told Lucinda about his boating accident, and about waking up in Moses Weisman's bed. He told her about Violet, about her tonette, about the music lesson.

"She sounds like Clarabelle with a more extensive vocabulary," said Lucinda. "Why don't you make some *normal* friends, Nathan?"

"Violet reminds me of my daughter," said Nathan. "And Moses is like a father to me. After only two days we are very close. I'm extremely fond of both of them. Moses is dying of cancer, Lucinda. I feel a need to care for them."

Lucinda told Nathan all about her plans to propel Eric Angstrom into the rarefied stratosphere of Dallas avant-garde art. Following the close of D'Amato's pivotal (and highly-acclaimed) show, and allowing time to re-plaster the walls and refinish the floors, Lucinda's Dallas Gallery of Modern Art would launch a massive one-man exhibition of some two hundred and fifty blank photographs.

"Don't you think one would suffice?" Nathan asked.

"They are actually all different, Nathan. You haven't looked at them. Eric has achieved an amazing variety of subtle hues and textures. He's an exquisite craftsman. An absolute *wizard* in the darkroom! He told me he makes at least *fifty* prints for every keeper! Eric is an *incredible* perfectionist!"

"He sounds like a Kodak salesman's wet dream to me," said Nathan. "Where does he get the money for all the paper and chemicals? And the time? Does he have a job?"

"Yes. He told me he works for Larry Proffitt."

"Larry Proffitt?! A neo-nihilist working for a slimeball faith healer? Now I've heard everything! What is he, a telephone prayer minister? An urban outreach missionary? WHAT?!!"

"*I* don't know, Nathan. Calm down. I'm just telling you what he told me. The important thing is that he has what he needs to create his art."

"Bullshit!" said Nathan. He rolled over, turning his back to Lucinda, and lay awake angry. However, the residual undulations of the waterbed caused by his violent movement had a calming effect on him, rocked him to sleep and into a pleasant dream of roller-skating with Violet, hand in hand, around White Rock Lake.

NINETEEN

The next morning, after making his regular urine delivery to Dr. Smith's office, Nathan stopped by a sporting goods store to buy a pair of roller skates. He asked for the old-fashioned kind with metal wheels, ones that would clamp onto the soles of his shoes, but he was superciliously informed by a teen-aged clerk that "they haven't made those things since World War II, Sir." The clerk tried to sell him an expensive and dangerous-looking pair of "rollerblades," but Nathan wisely declined and settled instead on a conservative pair of black lace-ups with "SpeedBall" fiber wheelsets. With butterflies in his stomach, he paid for the skates and left the store, now equipped to make his previous night's dream come true.

On the spur of the moment, Nathan decided to stop by the Michael Davidson Fashion Photography Studio to say hello to Michael-Michelle. When he walked in he found her sitting on the powder blue leather sofa in the reception area. Sitting beside her was Eric Angstrom. He had his hand up Michael-Michelle's frilly pink dress, but quickly withdrew it as Nathan came in the door.

"I'm sorry," said Nathan. He turned around immediately to leave.

"Nathan, wait!" cried Michael-Michelle, jumping up and straightening her clothes. "It's all right!" She ran to him and stopped him. "Don't go. It's O.K."

"I'm sorry. I shouldn't have barged in like that," said Nathan.

"I'll be in the darkroom," said Angstrom sullenly. As he walked past them and disappeared into the darkened studio behind the partition, Nathan saw that he had a rather formidable erection.

"What's going on, Michelle?" Nathan felt irrationally angry, a feeling not unlike the insane jealousy he had felt when his ex-wife Nancy had shown him the picture of Jimmy McCracken in the "Personalities" section of the *Richmond Times-Dispatch*. "What are you doing with that creep?"

"Eric is not a creep, Nathan. I like him."

"Does he . . . does he know that . . . ?"

"Yes, he knows. Eric is gay, Nathan. And he's very sweet. A bit morose, but very kind and gentle. I think I have finally found someone who can love me for what I am."

Nathan sat down on the sofa and put his head in his hands. He began to cry.

"Nathan, what's wrong?" Michael-Michelle sat down next to him and put her arm around his shoulders. "What is it?"

"I don't know," he sobbed, "but for some reason . . . I feel . . . I think I feel jealous."

"Nathan, Eric has nothing to do with *our* friendship. We will *always* be friends, no matter what." She comforted him, dried his tears with her soft white hands, which smelled faintly of gardenias. She held him and kissed him on the forehead. "Please be happy for me. I think I love him."

Nathan got control of himself, sat back a bit to separate from her. He felt slightly uncomfortable being that close to her physically.

"What is he doing in your darkroom?" Nathan asked.

"Oh, I'm letting him use a special mural enlarger I have. He wants to make a ten-by-twelve-foot print of one of his photographs . . . 'The Absurdity of Space' . . . I think that's what he calls it."

"Michelle, you don't buy that nihilist bullshit, do you?"

"I'm a fashion photographer, Nathan. A craftsperson. I'm not an art photographer. The only art I understand or care about is dancing. I don't care what Eric does, as long as it makes him happy."

"It doesn't make him happy. It makes him miserable. And he's trying to make everybody else miserable, too."

Michael-Michelle changed the subject. "I have some bad news, Nathan."

"What?"

"Geronimo was arrested last night for attacking some man in front of that . . . that living center where you're staying."

"La Coterie?"

"Yes, that's it."

"My God! Where is he now?"

"He's at Parkland Hospital. Some old man split his head open with a stick. A security guard, I think. He's going to be all right. He called me this morning. I'm going to visit him later today. He sounds terribly despondent."

Nathan raced to Parkland in his Toyota.

The top of Geronimo's head was completely bandaged. He looked like an Indian from India wearing a turban. He had a mild concussion.

"Geronimo, what the hell's the matter with you? You're going to wind up in prison!"

"I was sure it was Corporal Williams, Kemosabi."

"Corporal Williams is probably in Toledo, Ohio, for Christ's sake! Or Charleston . . . or San Diego! What makes you think he's even *in* Dallas?"

"I thought it was him."

Geronimo wouldn't talk to Nathan. He was deeply depressed.

And he had a major hangover.

Nathan drove in a fury to La Coterie.

He stormed into the gatehouse.

"So much for your civility and kindness bullshit!" he shouted at Pops. "You goddamned old hypocrite!"

"Nathan, I had to! He was about to *kill* the poor guy! He'd ripped his pants off! He was trying to cut his balls off."

"Well, you didn't have to call the police!"

"I didn't, Nathan! It wasn't me!"

"Who did, then? The guy he attacked?"

"No, it wasn't him. He took off running half-naked toward the symphony center screaming his head off. I think he was a tourist. He's probably still running. I don't know who called the cops. The concert was just letting out at the time it happened. Hell, half those people saw the whole thing. I guess it was one of them."

Nathan forgave Pops for splitting Geronimo's head open again, realizing that he had probably done the huge Apache a favor by preventing him from mutilating or murdering an innocent tourist. They had a couple of snorts of gin and tried to figure out what they could do to help their friend. Short of having him committed, they couldn't think of anything, and Nathan was against that idea.

At noon, Nathan took back his Kurt Vonnegut novels and left to go see Violet.

"Where you headin' now?" Pops asked him.

"Going roller-skating, Pops."

"Atta boy, Nathan!"

When Nathan arrived at the Weisman's house, Violet was already out skating alone. Moses was up and was having a good day, so Nathan sat with him in the darkened living room, and they talked. Nathan told him what had happened to Geronimo. Moses listened with his eyes closed as Nathan related the sad story, and remained silent for a long while after he had finished. Nathan thought he had fallen asleep. Finally he spoke.

"Geronimo Jones is one of the more visible victims of our society," Moses said. "But you, Nathan . . . and millions of others like you . . . have also been victimized . . . slowly and insidiously poisoned by American culture . . . a smiling and apparently innocuous culture, but a cold-hearted, spirit-killing brute nonetheless."

Moses got up from his easy chair and went to the window. Nathan could see tears in his eyes, glistening in the harsh light coming through the panes.

"Anna and I were also brutalized, of course, but in a different way. Our horror came suddenly, unexpectedly, and with deadly certainty. We knew what was happening to us, and we could do nothing to stop it."

He turned and faced Nathan.

"The difference is . . . is that you . . . and most of the other poor souls in this country . . . have never truly realized what was being done to you."

"How can you compare American culture to what you and your wife suffered? What you went through was . . . *unthinkable*! Americans are just bored!"

"That may be true, Nathan. But in the end, misery is misery . . . suffering is suffering . . . and death is death."

Moses came back across the room and sat down on the sofa next to Nathan.

"In any case, Anna and I escaped the darkness of *our* lives by dancing. And so can you, Nathan. So can you!"

"I don't dance, Moses. I've never danced."

"That's because you don't know how, Son. Let me teach you. I promise it will change your life."

"But . . . what kind of dancing? I'd feel silly, Moses. I'm nearly fifty years old."

"Tap-dancing, Son! Tap-dancing! It's the happiest dance there is! Pure spontaneity! Pure feeling! Pure fun!"

"I don't know, Moses."

"Please, Nathan. Let me show you how. I can *teach* you! And juggling, too! Haven't you ever wished you could juggle?"

"Yes. Yes, I have," said Nathan. Moses' enthusiasm was contagious.

"Good! I'm a great juggler! And so is Violet! We can teach you! It's easy!"

"Violet juggles?"

"You bet she does!"

"Does she tap-dance, too?"

"One of the best! She's totally uninhibited!"

"By God, you're on, Moses! The truth is, I've always wanted to tap-dance!"

Moses beamed at Nathan, flung his old bony arm over his shoulder.

"You know, Son," he said in a low, confidential tone, "I think some people in this world were meant to work. And I believe some were meant to lead. But a few of us, like Violet and me . . . and *you*, Nathan . . . we were meant to *dance!* To *juggle!* To pursue *whimsy!* What else can we do?"

When Violet came in, hot and sweaty from roller-skating, she found Nathan and her wheezing father equally hot and sweaty from tap-dancing and juggling. Moses was a good teacher. Nathan already had a few basic steps down, and he delighted Violet with a demonstration. Then Violet dazzled them both with a spontaneous dance, freely improvised from her childlike spirit and without even a trace of self-consciousness.

That evening, Nathan prepared dinner, then later washed the dishes while Violet and Moses dried. He showed Violet his new roller skates, much to her excitement, and helped Moses tuck her up after she had taken her bath and put on her pajamas.

After Violet had gone to sleep, Nathan practiced his scales while Moses grumpily read the paper, griping and complaining about the idiocy of the Dallas City Council.

For the first time in his life, Nathan knew true contentment.

TWENTY

Over the next two months, Nathan spent nearly all of his time with Moses and Violet. Lucinda was busy mopping up after the D'Amato show, and she was distracted by all the details of setting up the Angstrom exhibit. Nathan discovered that Lucinda had never actually heard of neo-nihilism either. It turned out that much of her excitement over Eric's strange and melancholy work was because of the possibility that she might go down in the art history books as the first person to recognize and give credence to an entire new *movement*, rather than just another solitary genius.

Michael-Michelle was happily dating Eric and helping him print his infinity-snubbing murals. Nathan had lunch with her a couple of times at the Pasta Emporium, but that was it.

Geronimo Jones remained distant and non-communicative after his attack on the hapless tourist. Since no one had filed charges, he was released from custody following his discharge from Parkland. Nathan stopped by his seedy apartment one day to check on him, but he was drunk and belligerent. One Saturday night, Nathan went to The Cockpit to talk to him, to try to offer his help in some way. Skinner met him out front and told him that Geronimo had shown up drunk the week before and that he'd fired him.

"You're a heartless son of a bitch," Nathan told him. "You summarily dismiss a faithful, long-time employee the first time he slips up. You have the best father a man could want, and you spit on him. You have a sister who desperately needs a brother to love her and care for her, and you completely ignore her."

Nathan thought he would get a dramatic reaction from Skinner when he made it evident that he knew Moses and Violet, but it didn't seem to faze him. Nathan figured Moses must have told him about their relationship.

"As far as Geronimo is concerned," said Skinner, "he doesn't need this job. He's rolling in money from selling his piss to Smith. As far as Moses is concerned, he's crazy as a loon, and he's never done a day's work in his life. If he's not doing some stupid dance, he's juggling grapefruit. And as far as Violet is concerned, she's my *half*-sister, and she hasn't got sense enough to come in out of the rain. She ought to be in an institution. And as far as *you're* concerned, Smartass, why don't you just mind your own fucking business?"

Nathan tried to take a swing at him, but as he drew his fist back, his anus cramped, and he fell to the sidewalk in agony.

"You're hopeless, Doering," Skinner said disdainfully. "Move along. You're blocking the entrance."

Nathan went roller-skating nearly every day with Violet. He was becoming more and more proficient at improvising on the piano, and the quality and depth of their communication was increasing daily. They went for long, silent walks in the woods. They played tag and hide-and-seek among the trees and bushes around the house. They made mud pies. They sat on the bank of the lake together and fished and watched the sailboats. Nathan was a happy man. It felt just like having a daughter of his own.

Moses' health rapidly deteriorated during those two months. Nathan began doing all the cooking and shopping and laundry and other household chores. He started spending most nights on the sofa in the living room. Moses refused to go to a hospital or even to see a doctor. But Nathan persuaded Dr. Peter Smith to get him some morphine to ease the old man's pain. Most of Nathan's long conversations with Moses were now at his bedside.

One evening, after a particularly bad day, Moses asked Nathan to bend down close so that he could hear his weak, wheezing voice clearly.

"I'm about to go, Nathan," he said. "Any day now."

"I know, Moses."

"I want to recite some poetry to you," he said. "This is from John Milton's poem *L'Allegro*. Listen:

> *Haste thee, Nymph, and bring with thee*
> *Jest, and youthful jollity,*
> *Quips and cranks, and wanton wiles,*
> *Nods, and becks, and wreathed smiles,*
> *Such as hang on Hebe's cheek,*
> *And love to live in dimple sleek;*
> *Sport that wrinkled Care derides,*
> *And Laughter holding both his sides.*
> *Come, and trip it as ye go*
> *On the light fantastic toe,*
> *And in thy right hand lead with thee,*
> *The mountain nymph, sweet Liberty."*

"Thank you, Moses. I liked that."

"Pursue whimsy, Nathan," he rasped. "Be joyful unto life. Care for Violet. She can teach you much. She can free you from the final burden . . . if you will let her . . . the burden of language."

"That's what you meant when you said Violet's deafness was a blessing, isn't it, Moses? I think I understand now."

Moses smiled weakly, closed his eyes, and drifted off to sleep on his downy pillow of morphine.

On the day of Eric Angstrom's opening, Moses seemed to rally. He was up and about, poking into things, complaining about Nathan's rearrangement of the kitchen cabinets.

Nathan decided to seize this opportunity to move out of La Coterie. Moses stopped him as he was leaving the house. He handed him a sealed envelope.

"Don't open this until I'm dead," he said.

Nathan put the envelope in his pocket and drove to the Arts District.

When he let himself into Lucinda's kitchen, Baby Bow Wow charged him and bit his leg. Nathan had been absent for so long that Baby Bow Wow mistook him for an intruder. Or had he? wondered Nathan as he writhed on the parqueted floor, his anus locked in an excruciating spasm.

Upstairs, Nathan packed his things. He decided to take one last glorious shower under Lucinda's high-tech Massage-O-Matic showerhead. He stood with his eyes shut under the warm, pulsating water for twenty minutes and nearly went to sleep on his feet. As he stepped out of the tub to dry himself off, he was startled by the sight of his own reflection in the full-length mirror on the bathroom door. He moved up closer and carefully studied his body. It was the first time he had really looked at himself in months. He could see a definite loss of muscle tone in his shoulders, chest, and arms. And his buttocks were looking fatty. They seemed softer, more rounded, and little dimples were beginning to appear. He poked his cheeks with his fingers. They sank in deeply, meeting little resistance. He was, for sure, becoming pear-shaped. And there was a decided loss of body hair.

Nathan brushed his teeth and got dressed. He didn't need to shave, so he didn't. He looked again at himself in the minor.

"I'm a eunuch," he said aloud to himself. "And that's O.K. with me."

As a symbolic act of assertion of his new self, he decided to urinate in the toilet for the first time in three months. But when he lifted the seat, something unfamiliar caught his eye. It was a long, red pubic hair on the porcelain rim of the toilet, curving in a sinuous line in the form of a question mark. It seemed to ask the question, "From whose virile plumage did I fall?"

Nathan tried to picture a fiercely masculine man with huge red furry balls urinating in the toilet after making passionate love to Lucinda in her waterbed. He tried to imagine how the hair, dislodged from its follicle by orgasmic friction, had floated down from his wild pubic patch in a graceful helix, like a winged maple seed on an autumn day.

The only redheads Nathan could think of were Jimmy McCracken, the girl at the lake with breasts like weapons, Eric Angstrom, and, of course, his urologist Dr. Peter Smith.

Well, this is certainly an enigma, thought Nathan. Jimmy McCracken was by all odds still in Richmond, Virginia, probably paying the bills for his daughter Rose's wedding about now. Nathan briefly tried to visualize the titanic-titted girl locked in Lesbian embrace with Lucinda, but the image vaporized before it had fully formed. Improbable at best, he concluded dreamily. Eric Angstrom? He was gay. Bisexual? Perhaps. But not likely, thought Nathan . . . and that leaves only Dr. Peter Smith . . . and no *way* would Lucinda make it with a flamingo!

Nathan let his urine go, aimed his golden stream at the taunting hair, knocked it off into the bowl, then flushed the whole vaguely disturbing business down into the devouring bowels of the great city of Dallas . . . the city with a large intestine as big as the heart of Texas.

Casting one final glance around the bedroom, Nathan noticed that he had forgotten to pack his copy of Tristan Jones' *The Incredible Voyage*, which was lying on the bedside table. He tossed the book in his suitcase, latched it, and descended Lucinda's stairway of love and torture to the living room.

As he was about to remove his testicle from under its little bonneted duck tea cozy, the phone rang. It was Michael-Michelle, and she was weeping.

"Oh, Nathan," she sobbed. "Something terrible has happened. I've been trying to call you for five days. I couldn't find you. Lucinda didn't know how to reach you."

"What is it?" Nathan cried. "What happened? Are you all right?"

"It's Geronimo . . . . He's dead, Nathan. Oh, God . . . it's so terribly tragic."

"What . . . how?"

"He killed himself, Nathan. Oh, God! I knew he was going to do something to himself! And I didn't do anything to help him!"

"Calm down, Michelle. It's not your fault. Nobody could help Geronimo. Tell me what happened."

Michelle described to Nathan the peculiar but somehow predictable events and circumstances that led to Geronimo's suicide. She said that Geronimo had been arrested by the police in downtown Dallas after they received a complaint that a fat man dressed only in a loincloth and fringed Naugahyde bedroom slippers had shot an arrow into the nose of a stuffed moosehead hanging over the entrance to the Moose lodge next door to the First Baptist Church. They had found Geronimo several blocks away, drunk as a skunk, savagely chopping at parking meters with a gaily-painted souvenir tomahawk he had purchased from the Cherokee reservation gift shop in Oklahoma. He was easy to spot. His pear-shaped, nearly naked body was painted, war-party style, in phosphorescent Day-Glow magic marker. He glowed in the dark.

The cops beat him up and threw him in jail. They confiscated his weapons and held them for evidence, but they were not needed after all. Geronimo hanged himself in his cell at sunrise the next morning.

"I buried him yesterday, Nathan," said Michelle. "I gave him a nice, dignified funeral. I'm so sorry you couldn't be there. I really did try to find you."

"I'm sorry, too," said Nathan.

"He left a note for you."

"A note? Do you have it with you?"

"Yes . . . but . . . Nathan, it's almost too heartbreaking to read."

"Read it to me, Michelle."

Nathan could hear Michael-Michelle struggling to control her weeping over the phone.

"Michelle. Please . . . read it to me."

"Dear . . . Dear Kemosabi: Please forgive me for disappointing you. I know you care for me. But I can no longer go on living in the white man's world. We gave our land away for trinkets. We traded our primitive but workable spiritual culture for Christianity. We exchanged our minds and our souls for television. And now I have committed the final outrage against my ancestors. I have sold my piss to the paleface so that I could have more money to buy forgiveness from a false god who hates me and will not give me peace at any price. I love you, Kemosabi. Good-bye."

"Thank you, Michelle. I'll talk to you later."

"Nathan, what did Geronimo mean about selling his . . , his piss to the paleface?"

"I'll talk to you later, Michelle."

Nathan calmly hung up the phone.

"PROFFITT!!!" screamed Nathan.

"YAHWEH!!!" barked Baby Bow Wow. He was startled awake by Nathan's voice. Nathan watched him with smoldering eyes as he ran in place under the dining room table, a blur of tiny legs, laying down hundreds of fine scratches with his sharp little claws on Lucinda's polished hardwood floor. He watched Baby Bow Wow's shiny black balls bobble absurdly between his muscular hindquarters as he gained momentum and shot, with a vicious snarl, through his little trap door in the kitchen . . . *flappity, flap-pity, flap . . . flap.*

Nathan ran out of the condo, jumped in his car and left La Coterie. As he passed through the gate, Pops leaned out of the gatehouse window.

"Where you off to now, Nathan?"

"To settle a score, Pops!"

"Atta boy, Nathan!"

TWENTY-ONE

Nathan went to a sleazy camera store in downtown Dallas that had diversified by also offering an assortment of automatic assault weapons, shotguns, and pistols over the counter to any nut who might walk in with enough money. Nathan the nut walked in and plunked his money on the counter. He selected a relatively inexpensive revolver and asked for one bullet and one blank only. The clerk, watching him suspiciously, told him he had to buy them by the box, or not at all. Nathan paid and left the store feeling feverish.

His next stop was a discount carpet outlet. He bought a narrow eight-foot long foam rubber pad designed to cushion a hall runner carpet. Next, the drugstore, where he bought a little dispenser of waxed dental floss, extra-fine.

He raced back to La Coterie, took the carpet pad into the condo and carefully laid it out, placing one end where Baby Bow Wow always slept under the dining table. The other end of the pad he pointed directly at the flap in the kitchen door. Carefully checking the placement and angle of the pad one last time, Nathan hurried back out to his car.

He drove to Lucinda's gallery, slipped into the courtyard, and hid behind the quasi-cubist scrap metal representation of male genitalia. He peeked around the sculpture into the gallery windows until he could determine the exact whereabouts of Lucinda, who was busily putting the final touches on Eric Angstrom's absurd exhibition.

When he saw he could make it without being detected, Nathan sneaked quickly into the gallery and into Lucinda's private office. With trembling, sweaty hands he flipped through Lucinda's record books until he found the address of Brother Larry Proffitt, the dark pope of perversion, fornography, and pornication. As Nathan expected, he lived in one of the tacky, two-million-dollar mansions in a new, upscale subdivision developed in far North Dallas by none other than Thaddeus Raven, the Dallas Arts District visionary and King of Suburbia.

Nathan sneaked back out to his Toyota and, consulting his Mapsco, sped northward to his meeting with destiny and the cold-blooded killer of Geronimo Jones.

Nathan found Brother Proffitt's house easily. It was the only one on the block with soaring cathedral ceilings and stained-glass windows. He parked in the alley behind, climbed over the high wooden privacy fence into the back yard, and ran toward the darkened house. In his mad dash toward justice and revenge he grew careless and tripped over a lawn sprinkler, nearly falling into Brother Larry's cruciform swimming pool.

As if by an act of God, the back door was miraculously unlocked. Nathan stole in, pistol in hand, and crept from room to room, looking for his evil target. The lower level of the house was deserted. As he tiptoed near the broad, winding staircase, he heard muffled voices from above. Slowly, breathlessly, he ascended the carpeted stairs. As he approached the landing, the voices became clearer. One in particular.

"Kashanda! Boh-tanda! Oh, YES, Lord! Banish the demons of iniquity and filth from my lustful, pornicating, voluptuous body!

Ohhh . . . ! Sweet GEE-zus! Let me FEEL your healing hand ah-PONE me!"

Then Nathan heard a series of sharp, slapping sounds, intermixed with loud yelps and wails, which were followed by another vaguely familiar voice.

"You filthy bitch! You disgusting, nasty little cocksucking harlot! Take *that*!"

SLAP . . . SLAP . . . SLAP.

"You've been a *very* naughty girl, haven't you, Mary Magdalene?"

SLAP . . . SLAP . . . SLAP . . . SLAP . . . .

Nathan crept quickly to an open door where a soft lavender light spilled out onto the plush carpet of the hallway. He peeked around the doorjamb and witnessed, to his everlasting astonishment, Brother Larry Proffitt dressed in a lavender satin gown, lying, with hairy buttocks exposed and inflamed, across the lap of a totally naked man who was a dead ringer for Jesus Christ. The naked man was, of course, Eric "The Red" Angstrom, neo-nihilist artist of the absurd and acolyte of Marquis de Sade.

"SPANK me, Jesus!" wailed Brother Larry. "I am a slut! An obscene, perverted, pornicating whore! I have sinned! Ohhhh! SPANK me! SPANK me, Jesus! SPANK the demons of perversion out of my filthy little bottom!"

SLAP . . . SLAP . . . SLAP . . . SLAP . . . SLAP . . . .

Nathan noted with interest that a home video camera on a tripod was documenting the entire religious exorcism of the demon-possessed Brother Larry Proffitt, a.k.a. Mary Magdalene.

Suddenly Angstrom stood up, dumping Larry-Mary rudely on the floor, satin skirt askew.

"That's it, Proffitt. Your time is up. I've got to get to my opening. Give me my money."

Brother Larry stood up awkwardly and hobbled over to the video camera on his matching high-heeled lavender pumps. He flipped off the camera and kicked off his pumps. His little snake face was as red as his filthy little bottom. He went to his bureau and picked up a wad of bills. Eric, who had quickly dressed, strode over and roughly grabbed the money out of Proffitt's tiny pink fist.

"Well, I enjoyed it, as usual," said Brother Larry. "I hope you did, too, Eric."

"*Enjoy*? Don't flatter yourself!"

"Well, then God bless you, my boy, for indulging my harmless, silly little eccentricity. I will pray for you."

"Yeah, sure. You do that, Mary. And I'll pray for you, too."

"Don't blaspheme the Lord our God!"

"He may be *your* god, Bubba Larry, but he sure as hell ain't mine!"

"Eric, I *asked* you not to call me Bubba! Why are you so angry? Why must you be so sacrilegious?"

"Look, you sick-o pansy Jesus freak! You do this for kicks! I do it for art! The money you pay me to spank your ass goes to buy the film, chemicals, and paper I need to make my photographs. That's how I justify it! How do you justify it? You fucking hypocrite!"

Angstrom stalked out of Brother Larry's den of iniquity. Nathan pressed his pear-shaped body as flat as he could against the wall outside the door and held his breath. Angstrom never knew he was there. When Nathan heard the front door slam shut downstairs, he cocked his pistol and entered Bubba Larry's whore's bedroom. It was all done in lavender tones, reminiscent of the erotic ambiance of The Lavender Ballroom.

"Welcome to hell, motherfucker," said Nathan devilishly.

Brother Larry, who was bent over, clumsily trying to get out of his gown, jumped four feet in the air and fell in a tangled, satin mess on the floor. Nathan relished the expression of stark terror on his face as he pointed the pistol between his snake-like eyes.

"Your pompadour looks like you've had Philistines fighting in it," said Nathan.

"Please! Please don't shoot me!" begged Brother Larry, shedding real tears for perhaps the first time in his entire corrupt life.

"You know, Bubba, I'd really like to plug ya, but as a cowboy once said in an old Indian massacre movie, you ain't worth a bullet."

"Then what do you want?' Larry blubbered. "Who are you?"

Nathan walked over to the video camera. He removed the cassette and held it up for Proffitt to see.

"What I want, and what I'm taking, is this documentation of who *you* really are. And who am I? I'm Beelzebub, Bubba, and I'd better not *ever* see your fucking face on television again! If you don't dissolve your Faith 'N Fortune racket immediately, I'll expose your filthy little bottom to the whole world. And if *that* doesn't stop you, I'll come back and cut your balls and half your dick off so you'll know how it feels to be Geronimo Jones!"

Nathan turned and walked calmly out of the room, leaving Brother Larry Proffitt on his knees and whimpering like a penitent Mary Magdalene in his satin gown, the wrath of God worming into his black heart, the vestigial blush from Angstrom's sadistic palm still smarting on his sanctimonious buns.

Nathan drove as fast as he dared toward Lucinda's gallery. He knew Michael-Michelle would be there, looking as pretty and feminine as ever, blushing with the glow of romantic infatuation for her knight in shining armor who, he felt desperate to warn her, might well harbor true sadistic tendencies even though he denied to Brother

Larry that he enjoyed it. Better safe than sorry, thought Nathan.

He screeched to a halt in front of the gallery and rushed in through the courtyard. In his haste, he cracked his head on what conceivably could have been the left testicle of the quasi-cubist scrap metal representation of male genitalia. He stumbled with dizziness but maintained consciousness through sheer will. His mission was too critical to faint right in the middle of it. He entered the gallery, wild-eyed, with blood trickling from a small but painful gash on his forehead. He looked around the crowded gallery, trying to spot Michael-Michelle.

"What the hell are you doing here?" Lucinda demanded furiously. Nathan had not even noticed her marching angrily toward him through the swarm of perplexed art patrons who were looking vainly for some recognizable image in the absurd sea of infinity that was Angstrom's art.

"I've got to find Michael-Michelle! It's an emergency!"

"You look like hell! Come in my office! *NOW!*"

Nathan obeyed. Lucinda shut the door firmly, resolutely.

"Nathan, I've been trying to find you for more than a week! Something has come up. We need to talk."

"I've got to find Michael-Michelle, Lucinda!"

"Shut up! Now listen to me! You've got to get out of my condo."

"What?"

"I'm getting married."

"*What?*"

"I'm marrying Dr. Peter Smith. Your urologist."

"WHAT?"

"I'm carrying his *child*, Nathan!"

Nathan stared at her dumbfounded.

He thought about the red pubic hair in the form of a question mark on the rim of her toilet, tried to imagine it floating down from Smith's weedy little pubic patch. The image wouldn't come together.

"He needs me," said Lucinda," . . . and I need him."

"Lucinda. He's a flamingo."

"Look, I realize that Peter is not very attractive physically, but I've come to know him as a very sweet, decent man."

"And rich."

"Yes. *Very* rich. Is that a crime, Nathan?"

"To be rich? No, not necessarily. Very rich? Yes, Lucinda, I would call that a crime."

"Well, I'm sorry you don't approve."

"Lucinda, what on earth can you possibly see in the man? You already have more money than you know what to do with."

"Peter has given me the one thing I've always really needed but never *knew* I needed. A baby, Nathan. A *baby*. It's the one thing you could never have given me."

"If you hadn't screamed so loudly the day I met you, I might just have given you what you didn't know you needed."

"It wouldn't have worked anyway, Nathan. You're almost fifty years old. By the time our child would have started kindergarten, you'd have been dead . . . with that temper of yours."

"Well," said Nathan, "I guess we can thank Baby Bow Wow for the ultimate contraceptive. I'll be out of your condo tonight. Good-bye, Lucinda."

Nathan left her office and rushed to find Michael-Michelle. He looked everywhere for her. He even checked the ladies rest room. Then, considering the possibilities, he checked the men's room. Finally, in desperation he ran out into the darkened sculpture garden, searching frantically among the erotic statues.

Suddenly, he heard a distinctive sound, a sound so deeply ingrained in his subconscious that he involuntarily reacted like a Pavlovian dog with a tiny twitch in his moribund penis: it was the beloved and unmistakable moan of female orgasm! He rushed blindly in the direction of its origin . . . and there, between the softly rounded inner thighs of the monstrous bronze statue of the nude woman, Nathan beheld his angelic Michael-Michelle and the sadistic Eric Angstrom copulating like wild animals on the ground.

"Michelle!" he shouted.

Michael-Michelle and Eric separated like opposing magnets, scrambling to straighten their clothes.

"Shit! It's him again!" said Angstrom through his teeth.

"Nathan!" cried Michael-Michelle. She saw the blood on Nathan's forehead as he rounded the statue in a rage. "You're hurt!"

"Michelle! You don't know what you're doing! You don't know who you're dealing with!"

"You know, Doering, you're starting to develop a very bad habit!" said Angstrom.

"Shut your fucking face or I'll shut it for you!" Despite his soft, pear-shaped body, Nathan could still be quite intimidating.

"Michelle, this guy's bad news! You've got to believe me!" Nathan pleaded.

"Nathan, listen to me," Michael-Michelle said calmly, looking steadily into his darting eyes. "I am deeply in love with Eric. And he loves me . . . just the way I am. Do you know what that means to me, Nathan? I won't have to go through with the operation."

"I'm going to marry her, Doering, if that makes you feel any better," said Angstrom, sounding rather like a young suitor talking to his future father-in-law.

"What?"

"It's true, Nathan!" said Michael-Michelle radiantly. "We're leaving for our honeymoon tomorrow. We're going to Denmark! We're going to actually get married!"

"What?"

"Oh, Nathan! I'm so happy! I'm truly happy for the first time in my life! Please don't spoil it."

Nathan stared at the young, happy couple. He looked back and forth, from one to the other. He felt befuddled. Finally, against his better judgment, he gave in. He said the only thing he could think to say.

"If you ever hurt her, Angstrom, I'll kill you."

He sounded rather like a future father-in-law.

TWENTY-TWO

Nathan drove in a white heat to La Coterie, his raging thirst for revenge still unquenched. He fingered the pistol and the extra-fine dental floss in his pocket and smiled fiendishly.

He turned into the gingerbread carport with his headlights off, killed the ignition, and got out of his car, shutting the door quietly. He walked quickly down the lane and around the corner, to the front door of the condo where he let himself in silently.

"Ahhh . . ," he breathed with relief, seeing that Baby Bow Wow was snoozing away on the foam rubber carpet pad he had so thoughtfully provided for his little friend.

"Nice doggy," whispered Nathan as he checked and saw that the dog's shiny black testicles were splayed out nicely, as they usually were. "Him was my widdle Baby Bow Wow," he cooed softly as he carefully extracted an eight-foot length of floss from its dispenser and snipped it off on the built-in cutter. He made a little slipknot, a kind of self-tightening noose, and approached the dog on cat's paws. Kneeling behind Baby Bow Wow, quiet as a mouse, he carefully positioned the dental floss loop over his inordinately large, nasty little nuts, and gently closed the noose around them, being ever so cautious not to tickle.

Nathan then tied the bitter end, so to speak, of the thin but super-strong floss tether to one of the legs of Lucinda's heavy oak dining table. He stood up, taking pains to avoid bumping his head on the table, and tiptoed into the living room. He sat down on the

Early American sofa and reloaded his pistol with blanks.

Suddenly the phone rang, sucking every last cubic centimeter of air from Nathan's lungs. He snatched up the receiver and looked with alarm over at Baby Bow Wow. Mercifully, the dog snoozed on, reacting with only a tiny twitch of his tethered testicles.

"Hello?" whispered Nathan into the receiver.

"Doering?"

"Yes?"

"This is J. Charleton Skinner, III."

"What do *you* want, dickhead?"

"This is no time to be a smartass, believe me. Why are you whispering?"

"What do you want, Skinner?"

"I have some good news and some bad news."

"Let me guess," whispered Nathan. "Smith's been busted by the FDA, and you're returning all my unsold piss to me."

"Very funny, Doering. What do you want first? The good news or the bad news?"

"Give me the bad."

"Moses is dead."

"I'm very sorry to hear that. Where's Violet?"

"She's asleep. She knows nothing. I'm here at the house with her."

"Good."

"Now for the good news. I am the executor of Moses' estate, and I . . . ."

"That's not good news for anybody, sleazeball."

"You don't want to fuck with me, Doering! You seem to forget that I'm a lawyer! And a damn good one!"

"Sorry. I don't want any more trouble," said Nathan. He had a big lump in his throat. He wanted to cry.

"O.K. Now for the good news. Moses has left you his entire estate, with the exception of The Cockpit, which goes to me."

"What?!"

"But there's one little condition: You must accept full, legal, lifetime guardianship of Violet."

"*What?!*"

"Don't make me repeat myself, Doering. Pay attention!"

"I heard you," said Nathan, his eyes filling with tears.

"Do you accept?"

"Yes. I do."

"Great! Now you need to get your butt out here as fast as you can and sign these papers. Your responsibilities start tonight. And make it snappy, Doering. I've got to be at The Cockpit in two hours."

"I'm on my way."

Nathan hung up the phone and pulled from his pocket the sealed enveloped Moses had given him that morning. He opened it and read the few short words the old man had scribbled in a shaky hand:

> "*Remember Milton's poem, Nathan. Dance the dance of life, and trip it as ye go. Dance for your very life, my son, and dance it all allegro! Love, Moses.*"

In a bleary daze, he picked up his suitcase and walked right on by Baby Bow Wow, into the kitchen and out the door, slamming it behind him. Before his foot touched down on the first step of the porch, he heard a muffled yelp from inside. A chill shot up his spine as he realized that Baby Bow Wow had hit the end of his dental floss tether.

He rushed back inside to see the dog hysterically streaking from room to room, slipping and sliding on Lucinda's polished hardwood floors, bouncing off the walls, running in little circles, growling and snapping at his empty scrotum.

As Nathan tried to approach him, Baby Bow Wow retreated fearfully to a corner of the dining room, cowering and whimpering pitifully. Nathan came closer, stooped, and tentatively extended his hand. He could not believe the transformation. The dog's eyes were now gentle and sweet, even loving.

Nathan reached closer to pat his head, and Baby Bow Wow licked his hand with his tiny pink tongue.

"I don't believe it," said Nathan. He gathered the trembling dog up in his arms, carried him up the stairs to Lucinda's bedroom, and put him gently down on the waterbed. He went into the bathroom and took hydrogen peroxide and a gauze bandage from the medicine chest. Back in the bedroom, he gingerly disinfected Baby Bow Wow's cleanly-snipped scrotum and made a little gauze diaper for him.

He stood back and looked affectionately at the dog. Baby Bow Wow stared back at him, adoringly.

"This is for the best, Baby Bow Wow," Nathan assured him, "even though I never would have done it to you if I'd been in my right mind. You're really a very lucky dog, you know? Testosterone only spells trouble, believe me. Life will be better now. Lucinda won't believe you're the same dog."

Nathan walked out of the room to the top of the stairs, then turned and looked back.

"Good-bye, Baby Bow Wow," he said.

Baby Bow Wow tried to wag his little bobbed tail and wound up wagging his entire body, causing Lucinda's waterbed to undulate gently.

Downstairs, Nathan picked up the pistol and the boxes of bullets and blanks that he had thoughtlessly left on the cobbler's bench coffee table. He put them in his pockets. In the dining room he removed the dental floss tether from the table leg and rolled up the foam rubber carpet pad.

Baby Bow Wow's inordinately large testicles were easy to spot. He picked them up off the floor and carried them to the mantle in the living room. He removed the little duck tea cozy from the jar of formaldehyde that contained his own once-precious lone gonad. He opened the jar and dropped Baby Bow Wow's balls into the breathtaking preservative liquid.

"Plop, plop . . . fizz, fizz," said Nathan whimsically. He closed the jar tightly, replaced the tea cozy, and left Lucinda's gingerbread condo forever.

As Nathan waited for the heavy iron security gate to open for him one last time, Pops MacDonald leaned out of his little gatehouse window.

"Where are you off to now, Nathan?"

"To trip the light fantastic, Pops! On my light fantastic toe!"

"Atta boy, Nathan!"

www.ingramcontent.com/pod-product-compliance
Lightning Source LLC
Chambersburg PA
CBHW031318120626
46554CB00001BA/458